MADE FOR MURDER

MADE
FOR
MURDER

Paul McGoran

NEW PULP PRESS

Published by New Pulp Press, LLC, 926 Truman Avenue, Key West, Florida 33040, USA.

For information contact:
Publisher@NewPulpPress.com

ISBN-13:978-0692499337 (New Pulp Press)
ISBN-10:0692499334

MADE FOR MURDER

PROLOGUE

MY NAME IS BAILEY VIEJO. I'm a detective on the Las Vegas police force, homicide squad. In twenty years on the force, I never worked a case with a higher profile than Sam Porter's. As you probably know, Shoo-fly was Sam Porter's nickname—and it became media shorthand for the wild hodgepodge of low crime and high society that made his story a tabloid sensation.

The case lingers long in the mind, partly because the personalities were so outrageous. From ex-con to grande dame, they stood out for the warped passions that drove them and for the ruthlessness in their hearts. Before it was over, six police departments had jurisdiction over the various charges of murder, felonious assault, embezzlement and mayhem that added up to Shoo-fly the scandal . . . Shoo-fly the media frenzy . . . Shoo-fly the criminal epic.

Christ, by the time we put it to bed I thought I was some kind of whiz-bang profiler adept at decoding the human condition. But that's all bullshit, like some crappy cable TV show with 'your host' pontificating about the motives of every murderous dickhead who snags a headline. You see, homicide detectives are like everybody else. Sometimes you think too damn much about your own little corner of the world. Which is when you begin to develop theories.

So why do I find myself chewing this one over in the silent recesses of the night? It's not the big-money players involved and not the glittery backstory of San Francisco and Newport society. It's not even the appalling sight of those violated corpses. What tortures me is the memory of the few moments I spent questioning Shoo-fly, when I looked into those

i

degenerate eyes telling me life had no value, that what I knew or didn't know was of no concern to him. I need to understand how you figure people like him; I need to understand how they get that way.

Telling you the story may bring me part way there.

CHAPTER 1

MOST MEN ARE GERBILS

HELENA SWANN DIDN'T HAVE to go out there in the desert where Mrs. Buckley lived. She could have transacted their business over the phone. But she was curious. Wanda Buckley was a local legend, a bawdy old woman Brad talked about when Helena was planning this little trip. Besides, she wanted off the Las Vegas Strip for a few hours, and a drive through the desert suburbs would be a welcome diversion.

It was Monday, and traffic had abated after the morning rush. Turning into Wanda's street, Helena saw the little sign out front: *Buckley Real Estate*. The house was pleasant enough, had that cut-rate 'villa' look so prevalent in the valley. As she stood by the front entrance and pushed the bell, the late morning sun assaulted her arms and legs.

A young woman in a lavender paisley halter-top and black shorts opened the door, a little mutt yapping behind her. Helena must have looked surprised—this couldn't be the old lady she was expecting.

The woman seemed to guess what she was thinking.

"Mrs. Buckley is just inside," she said, taking the dog by the collar and ushering Helena into the house.

A large matronly woman with a florid face lumbered into the living room and introduced herself as Wanda Buckley. She wore one of those telephone headpieces with mike attached, and was gesturing with the hand holding the cord.

"This here is a friend of mine, Lana Firewood," she

continued. "And the furry little guy is Don Juan."

Helena smiled at the name and turned to acknowledge Lana and the dog. "How do you do . . . both of you. If you don't mind my asking, why did you name him Don Juan?"

"Don't ask," Mrs. Buckley cut in. "The little humper may want to demonstrate."

She cackled over her own joke, and Lana snorted in spite of looking horrified. Helena forced a smile, not expecting a remark of that sort.

"Lana's just visiting while I take calls for my agency, Mrs. Swann. Reason I have friends over during the workday is because I'm an old woman who hasn't got a life worth tellin' about anymore. I like to hear what goes on in town, especially from a firecracker like Lana."

"C'mon Wanda, what is this lady going to think?"

"I suspect we all know what to think, darlin'," she said, looking Helena's way and raising a conspiratorial eyebrow. "Anyway, what can I do for you, Mrs. Swann?"

"I just dropped in to pay for the accommodations, Mrs. Buckley. The suite's lovely, by the way."

"Thanks," she said. "It's definitely better than your typical Las Vegas hotel room. Isn't it, Lana?"

"Wanda, you can stop that right now," Lana protested.

Mrs. Buckley was living up to Brad's description of her, a ribald battleaxe straight out of an Elmore Leonard novel.

Lana stood primping in front of a gilt-framed mirror over the fireplace mantel. Without looking at Mrs. Buckley, she began to speak in a familiar tone that suggested she was resuming a conversation started earlier.

"Just wait'll you see my new guy, Wanda. Tall, well-built like you wouldn't believe, and eyes that drill right through you. Wish I was more sure of him, but I guess that's part of the thrill."

"The thrill is he's a bad boy?" she asked.

"Maybe. You think I get fixated on that type?"

"I know you, girl. There's nothing like an out and out thug to make your heart go pitty-pat."

"M-m-m. I suppose. All I know is I intend to get him in tow. Even if I need Randy to help do it."

"What does Randy have to do with it? He's just a nice kid."

"That's the point, you know? Randy's *nice* and the new one . . . the new one gets jealous."

She laughed. "You are evil, Lana. Sometimes you make me wish I was still in the game."

"I suppose you know a little something about bad boys, Wanda."

"You *know* what I think. Most men are gerbils."

"And the ones who aren't gerbils? What are they?"

"Marlboro men or thugs, I guess."

Lana and Mrs. Buckley looked at each other and cracked up.

"Some choice," said Lana. "This one may be a little of both."

"I'm getting rid of a gerbil," Helena said, rising from the desk and handing a check to Mrs. Buckley. "I'm just now waiting for my final decree."

The old lady couldn't let that pass. "Maybe you'll find a Marlboro man before your vacation's over."

"A girl can always hope," Helena said. "Oh . . . there's one more thing. I have the place through Thursday, but I might leave early. Should I come back here to drop the key off?"

"Well, you could," she said, "but why inconvenience yourself? Just leave it at the front desk when you leave. They'll take care of it."

At the front door, Helena paused and said goodbye to the two women. All three exchanged the kind of small talk people make when they're unlikely ever to see each other again.

~ ~ ~

Driving towards town, Helena fell into brooding about her life and the mess she had made of it so far. This trip was a kind of anxiety vacation for her, a respite from San Francisco. She couldn't really afford it, but she needed the time alone. Still, she didn't want to be far from home if those divorce papers came through. Brad would want her back for sure to celebrate that particular good news.

Brad Styles was a constant in her life for as long as she could remember. Confidant, personal friend, executive director of her stepsister Angela's vast holdings—Helena couldn't remember when he wasn't part of her life, part of her family almost. Incredibly, they became lovers shortly after she left Jeremy. Incredibly, because they were practically brother and sister after so many years of close acquaintance.

This was no grand passion on her part, and yet Brad was the reason she was anxious for those divorce papers. He wanted to marry her. In all sincerity, she could look him in the eye and tell him she loved him, because she did . . . in her way. And knowing that his family fortune was the equal of Angela's didn't hurt in the least.

Helena should have been rich like Angela. But that dreadful word stepsister got in the way.Angela's father was one of the richest men in San Francisco. When he died, she was his sole heir. Despite the consideration Helena knew as his adopted daughter, Sam Sharples left his entire fortune to blood. Angela was very generous, but now Helena lived on handouts at her pleasure. The feeling she was a poor relation fed her insecurities, stoked her little rebellions and led to her unfortunate marriage. But all that represented the past, and this vacation was a step toward putting it behind her.

When you're in Las Vegas on a budget, people-watching becomes half your amusement, maybe more. On Tuesday night, a dark-haired fellow at one of the craps tables caught Helena's attention. People were swatting him on the back to urge him on. While he looked perfectly calm and self-assured, there was something unyielding, perhaps dangerous, about him. Tall and powerfully built, he would have stood out in any crowd. He wore a tailored gray suit, black wingtips, and a blazing white shirt, freshly starched. His tie looked hand-painted, the colors maroon and light blue. His only jewelry was a modest gold-tone watch.

At a venture, Helena strolled from the bank of nickel slot machines where she sat, and fit herself into the crowd surrounding the craps table. Immediately, he flashed a curious look her way. She glanced down to avoid eye contact, suddenly eager to place one last bet for the night. He was on a streak, so following his lead seemed the obvious choice. But she sensed he was due for a loss. And that was how she played it—ten dollars against the man.

Looking up, she caught him staring back, his disbelieving eyes accompanied by an insolent grin as he prepared to throw. All this in the half-second it took him to toss the dice and make his point. The crowd cheered and Helena walked away, ten dollars poorer and feeling a pair of wicked blue eyes burrow into her neck.

Outside, the night air was cool, and the Strip was ablaze in a gaudy tumult of streaming neon. The boulevard stretched north and south, the whole of it lit up large, blotting out all starlight with its corona of man-made tinsel. This was Las Vegas in all its cheap glory. As for Helena, she loved the look and the feel of the place. She wouldn't have been there otherwise.

Crossing the Strip on foot at the Monte Carlo, she continued straight through the commercial plaza in front of the building that housed her rented timeshare. The security guard looked up from his console and waved as Helena entered. In the elevator, she listened to the ding, ding registering each successive floor. Rising alone in that quiet space, she thought about the attractive man with the insolent leer playing craps and looking good in his gray tailored suit.

Inside the apartment, she tossed her bag on the foyer table and went directly to the big windows fronting the Strip. Gazing out at the traffic, she flipped open her cell phone and checked for messages.

There was just one. The voice was Angela's.

"Hi, Helena. Call me if you get a chance. Brad's back from Denver. And guess what? A package came today from your divorce lawyer."

Well there it was, the big news and her signal to start the celebration. So where was the thrill? After all, this meant marriage to Brad and a newer, cleaner lifestyle all her own. No matter—even though she couldn't charge into it with enthusiasm, she was still determined to have it.

CHAPTER 2

RAPID ATTITUDE CHANGE

MICKEY CULLION DIDN'T LIKE Las Vegas much, and didn't like the way his life was going. But he was the type to do anything for a friend. As if Shoo-fly was anybody's friend. Oh yeah, he liked him, couldn't say he didn't. So did a lot of folks, mostly the gals in town. Shoo-fly had a quick tongue and a bad boy charm, and he could be a lot of fun when things were going his way.

They shared a room at a rundown courtyard motel at the north end of the Strip where it turns kind of sleazy. Off and on, Mickey had been living with Shoo-fly Porter for about three years, and had known him before that in stir.

The lone bed was near the window overlooking the courtyard, and Mickey was lying there in his skivvies reading a magazine when he saw Shoo-fly out of the corner of his eye. He was snaking through the rows of parked cars, taking a diagonal route toward the stairs to the second floor balcony that the rooms gave out on. He had the easy long stride of an athlete, really a pleasure to watch. In a minute he pushed open the door to the room.

Right away, Mickey could tell he was agitated. He walked in real quiet, tossed his hat on the desk, took off his jacket and draped it over the chair. Then he turned, walked to the right side of the bed and sat down. After loosening his tie, he shook out a cigarette from a pack on the bedside table and fired it with a kitchen match.

Mickey figured what the hell, get it out into the open. "Well now, big guy, what's up?"

"Nothing."

"Can't be nothing, Shoo-fly. You're pissed off. Anybody can tell."

"Can it, Mickey. It's that little bitch, Lana. She didn't show up tonight."

"She, uh, told you she would?"

"No, but she always does on Tuesday. She's stepping out with that kid Randy she talks about."

"Hell, that's just to make you jealous is all. She's crazy about you."

"Funny way of showing it."

"Just let it go, Shoo-fly. Show her you don't fall for that routine."

He got up, still smoking, and began pacing the floor.

"I won't let her get away with it, Mick."

"Right, you don't have to. Just ignore her. She'll come calling."

Shoo-fly's upper lip stiffened in a sneer, his nostrils flared. He stopped pacing, stubbed his cigarette out, and stripped to the waist. Then he sat on the bed, his back to Mickey.

From long experience, Mickey knew he'd best shut up and wait. He tossed the magazine on the floor and shifted down in bed, lying there with his head propped up, keeping an eye on Shoo-fly. When he figured the storm had passed, he turned to switch off the bedside lamp.

Neither man said a word. The kind of silence that gets on your nerves.

The room wasn't totally dark because of light from the courtyard filtering through the window curtains. Mickey felt Shoo-fly make a quick turn onto the bed facing his back, not touching, but close enough so he could hear the big man breathe. When his left hand went to Mickey's thigh, he knew Shoo-fly was ready to pack all that tension into what passed for sex between them. He wouldn't say he didn't like it, because he never tried to stop him. But he was sure Shoo-fly didn't give a damn. Maybe it was release for him and maybe it was just to show he could take what he wanted whenever he wanted.

~ ~ ~

Next morning, Mickey was in the motel courtyard leaning against his old junk box, reading the paper and waiting for Shoo-fly to come down. He always took longer than Mick to get ready. Beyond the shave and shower, he put a lot extra into it. He was especially fussy about the way he dressed. Neither one of them had a lot of clothes, but Shoo-fly knew how to vary his look and keep his duds looking fresh.

Stepping out onto the landing from their room, Shoo-fly paused a moment and looked up to the clear, bright sky before heading down the outside stairs to the parking area. He was dressed in a dark sport jacket, tan slacks, and an open collar shirt. That quick stride of his carried him over to Mickey in no time.

Mickey pushed himself off the side of the car and folded his newspaper.

"I've gotta be at the bar by nine for my shift."

"Sure. Me, I'm gonna call in sick. How about letting me use the car? I'll fill the tank and spring for breakfast."

Mickey's eyes went wide and he gestured toward the car. "Lead the way, my man! Who the hell died and left you rich and independent?"

"Close. I picked up three grand shooting dice last night."

"Christ, Shoo-fly, you almost never gamble."

"Never for long, anyway. The percentages are lousy. Hey, do me a favor and cut the 'Shoo-fly' moniker. You're the only one who calls me that anymore. It's just Sam from now on."

"Whatever you say . . . Sam."

He got behind the wheel, backed out of the parking space, and drove to a diner type restaurant he liked just beyond Fremont Street. They were eating breakfast in a booth by the front window when guess who walks in but Lana Firewood with a slim, young, sandy-haired guy grinning from ear to ear.

Lana came through the door first. Mickey saw her glance around the diner before turning to speak to Smiley. He figured she must have spotted them, and he was holding his breath for what would happen next. Shoo-fly hadn't seen a thing yet.

She walked straight toward them, high heels clattering across the tiles, her boyfriend trailing behind like a happy puppy. Mickey thought to himself that a broad like Lana could make her presence known in twenty different ways. He looked up as she and Smiley came close, and she gave him a coy little wave while she still had Shoo-fly's back to her. Finally, she made a point of stopping and turning around when she passed them by.

"Oh hi, Sam!" she said, acting all surprised. "I almost didn't recognize you from behind."

Shoo-fly looked from Lana to Smiley, still chewing on a piece of toast. He nodded real quick and grunted. This may have been rude, but Mickey was glad he didn't speak, because it sure as hell would have been ruder. Lana looked annoyed, sort of squaring her shoulders and biting her lower lip.

"Good to see you, Mickey," she said, turning and swishing past with Smiley to an empty booth further along the aisle.

Shoo-fly put down his knife and fork, took the napkin out of his lap and tossed it on the table. His face was flushed.

"Come on," Mickey said, "don't let her get to you.

You know what she's doing."

"When I was a bouncer," he said, "I occasionally took a certain amount of pleasure in leaning on somebody who insisted on getting out of line. Pain is a terrific agent for rapid attitude change."

"She's trying to make you jealous, so forget it. Screw her."

"Screwing her is apparently one of the easiest and cheapest things to do in Las Vegas. Like being comped for a buffet lunch. I think both of them need a rapid attitude change."

"C'mon, man, take it easy."

Mickey was getting nervous and it showed. Shoo-fly took a deep breath and seemed to calm down.

"Listen, no rush Mick," he said, "but as soon as we're done here, I'll drop you off at work. I'm gonna take a long ride."

When Mickey asked him where to, he didn't answer. His face was set tight, and he stared straight ahead with a kind of dark expression Mickey couldn't even begin to fathom.

CHAPTER 3

LINGERING KISSES

LIEUTENANT VIEJO

NOT EVEN THE REPORTERS who crawled all over this case for months know that Sam Porter kept a kind of journal. Nothing formal—certainly not your leather-covered diary with lock and key. What we found later were two notebooks and some loose papers in Shoo-fly's handwriting that, taken together, fill in some pieces of the puzzle. Especially about that day in Las Vegas at Wanda Buckley's house.

It seems that Randy and Lana pulled up to Mrs. Buckley's home in the suburbs sometime around ten o'clock and parked in front. They had no idea Shoo-fly followed them. Lana was in the passenger seat. She pulled herself up close to Randy at the wheel and gave him a long, wet, tongue-searching kiss. Shoo-fly was ready to do them right there and then, whoever might see it be damned. There were red spots in his vision, and his breath came fast, but he shook it off. So he could do it right, he told himself.

He knew what was going on and that Lana had arranged it. It was Wednesday, and she always filled in for Mrs. Buckley by answering the agency phone line while Wanda took care of business in town. Shoo-fly knew because Lana had brought *him* there just a week before. She had given him the same kind of wet, lingering kiss that she favored Randy with today. He even remembered their conversation in front of the house.

"You know, Wanda's not home right now and I

13

could sure use some company," she had told him.

"Then use me, baby. I'm your boy!"

"O-o-o-o, it's a boy!" she squealed, moving her hand into his crotch and fondling his already stiff johnson.

Both of them were laughing. They rushed out of the car, met at the curb, and ran to the front door holding hands.

Today, however, Shoo-fly drove on to the new service road behind Wanda's house at the edge of the subdivision. A sort of wooded ravine separated the road from her neighborhood, and you'd never see his car from her place. He doubled back and climbed through the ravine and brush at the back edge of the property.

As he approached, he heard a dog barking inside. That meant Lana had walked over from her own place earlier, leaving Don Juan at Mrs. Buckley's before getting a ride from her into the city. Later, meaning now, Lana came back with a 'friend' for company, in time to answer the agency phone line. Same set up as last time with him.

It didn't take long for Shoo-fly to get into the garage and quietly jimmy the door to the kitchen. It was cool inside and a little dark. After hesitating a moment to look and listen, he walked to the kitchen island with the soapstone top, where he sat on a barstool and waited.

Lana and Randy had come into the living room through the front door. Shoo-fly heard her making baby noises to the dog and laughing with Randy. The television came on loud, nearly drowning out their conversation.

"The kitchen's right through there, Randy," he heard her say. "Why don't you get us a couple beers?"

As he pushed through the swinging door, Randy looked around for the refrigerator. Then his eyes locked on Shoo-fly, still sitting quietly on the stool by the kitchen island.

"Get out, son," he said in a low, even voice. "Just leave."

"Who the hell let you in?" asked Randy.

"It's real simple. I belong here, Junior. You don't."

"Really? Well, it's not like we're in competition, pal. Lana's been around the block. I'm here now, and I intend to get what I came for."

When Shoo-fly stood and moved toward him, Randy pulled a knife. The boy was nothing if not game. Shoo-fly grabbed his blade arm and stripped the knife away with his other hand. In close quarters, Randy tried to ram his knee into his crotch, but the big guy pivoted slightly and launched a right uppercut.

As Randy went down, his arm cleared the kitchen counter. Sprawled out on the floor, he reached for the wooden knife block that had tumbled down with him. Deftly, he withdrew a meat cleaver and rose to attack.

The first blow struck home, and Shoo-fly sustained a wicked defensive cut across the back of his left hand. But he sidestepped the second strike, twisted the cleaver out of Randy's grip, and knocked him down again with a right hand blow that crunched into his face and broke his nose. Blood and snot gushed out, and Randy was moaning, beaten. Shoo-fly felt his own blood rise inside him in a hot flood that set him tingling from head to foot.

"A cleaver, you fucking idiot!" he exploded. "I don't believe you went after me with a cleaver."

Poor Randy had to see it coming from the way Shoo-fly looked at him. The big man hefted the cleaver and hacked at him from the throat down, pausing only to kick his head in when Randy feebly raised his hands to make him stop.

Lana must have heard the racket, even though it was muffled by the blare from the television.

"Randy!" she yelled. "What's going on in there?"

Don Juan was yelping now in that hysterical way small dogs have. Shoo-fly scrambled out of sight to the side of the refrigerator. He was covered in flop sweat and his hair hung down on his forehead. Lana came through the door with the pooch trailing. She looked at Randy on the floor and all that blood, made a choking sound, and wobbled backwards. When she turned and spotted Shoo-fly, her eyes registered confusion, then relief—as if she were glad to see someone familiar, someone who could help. He held her eyes with his, moved to her in one stride, then snapped her slender neck before she could utter more than a puzzled whimper.

His brain on fire and red spots swirling in his vision, Shoo-fly picked up the cleaver again. He slashed through Lana's breasts and stomach, cutting her up like a chicken for a poultry shop meat case before wiping off his fingerprints and putting the cleaver in Randy's' right hand. Next he took up Randy's knife from the floor, yanked his trousers down, and sliced off his balls with the long, sharp blade. Again he stopped to wipe his prints and placed the knife in Lana's left hand. His staging didn't fool anybody later, but he got the weapons in the correct hand for each of his victims. Most important, he hadn't left any prints to incriminate himself.

After, Shoo-fly needed time to calm down. When his eyes cleared and his breath stopped coming in huge, gulping intakes, he took inventory of his person and immediate surroundings. It was sheer luck he didn't have a whole lot of blood on his clothes. He washed his hands, found a dishtowel to stanch the cut he had sustained, then wiped down every surface he had touched.

To get out of the house, he had to toe Randy's

lifeless body away from the kitchen door. Apparently, Don Juan scampered out after him, which he probably never noticed. In no time, he was back in his car on the service road.

CHAPTER 4

FATEFUL EXIT

AFTER THE NEWS FROM Angela, Helena Swann was buffeted with a mix of emotions, including exhilaration and dread. She was free now. Free to start a new life, free to paint the town, free to . . . marry Brad. Which was what she wanted, wasn't it? But the idea of another marriage was like a dark, looming cloud. Before even tasting freedom, she'd be in a cage again, fortune or no. Still, if she were honest about what mattered most, it was the security and stability that Brad could offer her.

When she awoke Wednesday morning, she decided to head home first thing. Despite her misgivings, she simply had to have a life that offered position and wealth, the power and prestige Dominick Dunne spoke of in that old cable series. If the shoe fits, why not wear it—flaunt it, even? Anybody else would.

She packed the two pieces of luggage she had borrowed from Angela and stuffed her overnight bag with her toiletries, makeup and lingerie. Before leaving the condo, she made a final pass around the living room and made sure the drawers in the bedroom were empty. Everything seemed in order, and she left for home.

Halfway to McCarran airport, she spotted the sign for the exit she had taken to Mrs. Buckley's house on Monday. With a start, she remembered the key for the condo suite in her purse. She might have called Mrs. Buckley and mailed the key from San Francisco, but she really wanted this off her mind. So she veered off the highway onto the exit in one of those split-second decisions you think about for the rest of your life.

Damn, she thought, I'd better not miss the early flight.

Soon Helena was pulling up to Mrs. Buckley's house for the second time in three days. She parked out front and walked down the driveway to the key drop. Lana's dog was outside and yapping randomly. That seemed odd, so she stopped and thought for a moment. Turning away from the drop, she placed the key back in her purse. When no one answered the doorbell, she picked up Don Juan to keep him quiet and carried him with her to the back of the house. There she noticed a door leading into the rear of the garage was ajar and felt something might be wrong.

Thinking to put the dog in a safe place and just leave, Helena peeked in. No car, nothing out of order. She nudged the door open further and slipped through.

Once inside the garage, she saw another door to what had to be the kitchen. It was open, just a little. That gave her pause; but Helena wasn't the type to panic. Standing still a moment, she listened, heard what was probably a television and decided to just poke her head in. If someone happened to be there, she'd say hello and that she had rung the bell without getting an answer. If no one was there, she would put the dog inside, get out and phone Mrs. Buckley. Or the police. Whatever.

She walked through the garage, her footsteps echoing sharply in the empty space. A moment later, her head was through the balky kitchen door—she had to push at it—and she was looking into hell. So much gore, so much blood . . . those poor dead bodies defiled in ways beyond her ken. She fixated on Lana's hair and clothes all matted and soaked red—and so unlike the carefully groomed girl she met two days ago. Still, Helena held herself together. Even when she figured out what was stuffed into the young man's mouth were his severed testicles.

She didn't scream or run. She just put poor Don Juan in that kitchen, reaching over the man's corpse at her feet and dropping the little fellow to the floor. The dog's nails went tapping across the tiles until he stopped and sat quivering in a corner by the sink. What stayed with Helena were the eyes. Their eyes, both Lana's and the young man's, were wide open, frozen in shock and surprise.

For now, all thought of the airport was gone. Helena had to determine how to react and what to do. Before returning to San Francisco, she must pull her act together. She wiped both doorknobs before leaving that awful place. Out in the backyard, she fished out a pair of sunglasses from her purse and put them on. Having gotten control of her emotions and mental processes as much as anyone could, Helena went back to her car and drove away.

What had she stumbled into? The best thing now was to be somewhere quiet, to sit calmly and think. The condo was still hers for the day, so why not go back? No one had observed her leaving earlier, no one had been at the security console—she could just keep her luggage in the car and return. As if she had been out for breakfast or something. Yes, that would work. She could stay there in her little perch over the Strip and figure out exactly what to do before heading home. The life Helena wanted would *not* be ruined before it even started by some ridiculous, sordid murder case that had nothing to do with her.

CHAPTER 5

A FAMILY PROBLEM

MICKEY CULLION WAS ALREADY at the motel when Sam came back that day. The boss had cut his hours down until he was averaging maybe four, five a day. Sam Porter walked in at two in the afternoon when Mickey had been there a half hour or so. It was easy to tell something was up. Sam looked pretty calm, but glassy-eyed, and he was chain-smoking. There was gauze wrapped around his left hand with some white tape over that.

Mickey didn't see the traces of bloodstains at first, but Sam's clothes were rumpled and askew, and there was this bulge in his jacket pocket. Which turned out to be a little towel with blood on it. Sam pulled the towel out and looked at it. That triggered something, and he laughed, a laugh that sounded like despair and exhaustion. Then he sat on the bed and talked about what happened at Wanda's place.

To Mickey it was scary, Sam repeating the same bad shit over and over, like a broke fuckin' record. When it all came clear, he figured the best he could do was try not to act upset, help him out as best he could.

"It was like I was in a time warp, Mick. I had this noise in my ears and my vision was fuzzy, and I got into the cutting and . . . and the blood. She never said a word, you know? But that punk, he talked. No more, though. I stopped that all right."

"You totally lost it, Sam," Mickey said. "Like before, only worse. This time you've gotta be smart and act fast. Both of us have to stay cool. Okay, pal?"

"Yeah. I get it."

They both knew the clothes had to go. Mickey told him to strip absolutely everything off so he could take care of getting it incinerated. Shoes and socks, and the towel too. All of a sudden, he was into it, figuring out what to do, helping him escape. What the hell did he think? That Sam would be grateful, or like him better? Probably that was it.

And Mickey was thorough, besides. He unwound the makeshift bandage and saw that Sam needed stitches. Not bad, but it had to be taken care of. This might be tricky, but making an emergency room visit with the right story should take care of it.

"You got all that dough from gambling last night, Sam, so what the hell, you can afford to go. Give them a phony name, tell them you was chopping up a chicken with a butcher knife and get a few stitches."

Sam nodded in agreement.

"Other than that, get cleaned up and get outta town."

San Francisco was where he would go, that very night. Mickey would stay in Vegas, go to work like usual. If Sam's boss called, he'd say he left for home with a family problem. Most important, he could keep his eyes open, read the newspaper like crazy, watch out for any sign the cops were looking for Sam. If they came by with questions for him, Mickey could judge whether they had a lead.

But nobody had a thing on him. That part he didn't have to worry about. How should he know where an ex-con like Sam Porter would go? He told me he was going home, officer, wherever that is.

Another thing they decided there in the motel room while Sam stripped off his bloody clothes was that Mickey shouldn't know exactly where he was staying. Every few days Sam could find a pay phone and call him at the bar, but until things were quiet, they wouldn't make any plans to reunite. The less Mickey knew the better.

Sam made a bundle of his clothes and shoes, wrapping it all up with his jacket and tying the arms together. Mickey knew just where to go when it got dark. There was an alley not far away where a few alkies would be tending a fire barrel.

Piece by piece in the darkness, the clothes flared up and disappeared. An old greybeard wino laughed like hell every time Mickey popped another article of clothing into the barrel. The shoes went in last, and somehow that made the old man mad. The poor bastard probably saw they were in better shape than the half-rotted sneakers he had on.

CHAPTER 6

A TRUE SCOUNDREL

HELENA SAT IN THE CONDO and thought hard about her predicament. When she was ready to leave, she had the beginning of a plan. She wouldn't be calling Mrs. Buckley about what she saw, and calling the police was out of the question as well.

This much she knew—it hadn't happened. She had seen nothing. Rather, she had packed her bags early, took a drive and went to breakfast. That was her entire morning. No one had seen her, she was sure. The whole thing was a non-event. For now, she would leave the key on the foyer table just as Mrs. Buckley had suggested. She would then go downstairs, say goodbye to the security guard, tell him she had put her luggage in the car earlier, and leave. Simple.

Helena made a change to her plan by the time she got downstairs and spoke to Irv, the good-looking young black man at the security console. It had occurred to her that she needed to spend time in bright, cheerful surroundings, somewhere near the bustle of commerce and people having fun. It would help her purge the gloom and charnel house images of that scene in the desert at Wanda Buckley's house.

She watched Irv type an entry into his computer screen.

"You're all checked out now, ma'am," he said, looking up and smiling.

"Great," she said. "I have a few errands to run nearby, so I'll come back later for the car. Thanks again for everything, Irv. I've had a *wonderful* vacation."

It sounded over the top to her own ears, but she

wanted Irv to remember her as a nice lady who was in good spirits when she left, not in the least upset or worried. Might be an important detail down the road.

"Bye, Mrs. Swann. Come back and see us some time."

Irv was a peach.

The Bellagio was within walking distance. Helena crossed the Strip on foot and mounted the moving sidewalk that rises into the hotel. Down and to her right, she watched the dancing fountains in the big pond outside performing choreographed magic to the brassy sound of Sinatra singing *Luck Be a Lady*. Once inside, Helena got the boost she needed from the color scheme, the lighting, and the fine shops with their luxury goods. Not that she wasn't still on edge—but her shattered mood had eased off, and she began to see her next move.

Some deep, rhythmic breaths as she strolled the thickly-carpeted mall concourse helped clear her head and keep her hands steady. Turning a corner, she found a quiet spot where two overstuffed armchairs and a small table inlaid with mosaic tile were framed and backlit by huge plate glass windows overlooking the lush hotel grounds and pool area. Helena sank into an armchair, facing out toward the parade of tourists flowing through the concourse. Day or night, there were always thousands of them.

She poked through her purse, pulling out a cell phone and a small notebook with pen attached. Her first call was for airline reservations. Most of the flights to San Francisco were booked, and she didn't care for her chances of getting stand-by seating. Finally, she settled for a reservation on a flight at ten twenty-five. That was late, but she could relax until then and treat herself to dinner at Le Cirque.

Her next call was to Angela, who would be

wondering why Helena hadn't raced home to see Brad and celebrate her divorce at the first opportunity. Telling her she needed to spend a relaxing extra day in Las Vegas wouldn't make any sense at all.

"Angela, honey, it's me."

"Helena, finally! I've been leaving messages all morning. I expected you home by now."

"I'll be in late tonight, Angela. I got your message last night about the divorce papers and shut my cell phone down afterwards. This morning I didn't turn it on since I was in a rush for the early flight home—which I missed. I haven't checked for new messages today because . . . I saw something this morning that frightened me, and I've been trying to sort it out ever since."

"You're upset. What's going on?"

"You can't even imagine."

Helena wasn't as upset as she sounded. That was a dodge, a little tune to set the scene. Having taken care to think things through, she was ready to tell Angela the truth. Well, almost. A half-truth here and there might help.

"My goodness, try to be calm and tell me about it." Angela sounded concerned and loving as always. She really did have all the virtues.

"I don't know if I can, but you have to know I'm all right. Nothing bad has happened to me. You know that woman Brad told me about, the one who rented me the suite here?"

"Certainly . . . Mrs. Buckley, Wanda Buckley. What about her?"

"I assume she's all right, I don't know. But I went out to her place this morning to return the key?"

"Yes . . . and?"

"What I saw there was pretty awful. But if I go to the police, I'll get caught up in some dreadful investigation."

"Helena, what in the world are you talking about?"

Here was the payoff. It had to be close to the truth, it had to be very good, and Helena would have to stick to it through hell and high water.

"There may have been a murder at that woman's house," she began.

"A murder! Oh, Helena."

Angela was with her now, for sure. Helena told her she had driven out to Wanda Buckley's place just before going on to McCarran airport, that she had forgotten to leave the key and decided to make the short side trip to her house and hand it to her in person. When Mrs. Buckley didn't answer the front doorbell, Helena looked for a back entrance because she could hear a television playing. Peeking into a kitchen window in back—there was one to the right of the garage, at a level Helena could have reached—she saw a body on the floor and fled the scene.

"Are you sure this person was dead?" Angela asked.

"No, honey, not sure, but I just couldn't stay there a second longer. When I thought of what to do, I almost called Brad, but you *know* how he is about publicity. Think of what his mother would say. I finally realized the best thing for me to do is nothing at all. Not a thing."

"That's beyond cold, Helena. It's criminal, even. Someone may be in real danger."

"I know I'm right, Angela. That person is either dead or alive. If she's dead, there is nothing in the world I can do for her. If she's alive, well, maybe Mrs. Buckley has found her by now."

"A woman? It was a woman?"

"Yes, I'm sure it was."

"Was there blood?"

"Quite a bit it seems to me. But I didn't linger at the

window. I got away quickly. You know, Angela, I could find a pay phone here and call Mrs. Buckley anonymously. To warn her, tell her not to go home without protection of some kind."

"It just might save her life."

"Really, Angela, I'm terribly upset about this. Is that something you could do? Find a pay phone in the city, not a phone they could trace, and tell Mrs. Buckley there may be trouble at home. Would you do that for me, honey?"

"I . . . I don't know."

"I understand. I shouldn't involve you. I'm nearly having a meltdown here."

"Well . . . maybe I *could* do it. Do you have her cell phone number?"

Helena was elated. Her story was so nearly true no one could ever disprove it, and she could count on Angela's assistance. With any luck, her problem was solved.

~ ~ ~

Once inside McCarran airport, Helena checked in and noticed Sam Porter on the concourse, playing quarter slots in a nonchalant, time-passing fashion. Where else but in Vegas would the airport be chock full of slot machines? After your week's vacation, the town is giving you one last chance to reverse your luck and go home a winner—or a loser. Porter was dressed as he had been the previous night in the neatly pressed gray suit and the shiny black wingtips. His shirt and tie were different, though—the shirt light blue, the tie black with gold and green swirls.

It took almost no effort to strike up a conversation. His eyes came up when she passed by. Had she slowed down to make him take notice? Of course she had..

"Remember me?" he said.

She nodded and smiled. "I could hardly forget you.

I lost ten dollars on that toss."

"You should have bet with me, not against me."

"Well, it was nothing personal. I just made a mental calculation that you were due for a miss."

"Really now?" he said, black eyebrows shooting upwards. "How long had you been following my action?"

He had her there. She admitted that the excitement surrounding his streak had attracted her, and that she watched for a minute or so.

"Well, why don't you give me a chance to make up that loss?" he asked. "I wouldn't want it said that a lucky streak of mine was the cause of grief for a lady like you."

That was pretty quick of him, and it wasn't the worst line she had ever been fed. They both knew it was a line, but the way he delivered it in that deep, husky voice gave him a lot of points in her book.

Helena and Sam remained together for the hour and a half before flight time. First, they stopped at a nearby bar adjacent to one of the seating areas and had a drink. They learned they were on the same flight, he in first class and Helena, unfortunately, in coach. There was a kind of tension between them, a level of excitement they both could feel.

They strolled the concourse for a time, slowly. Sam was very attentive to her, asking if she were comfortable, did she want a snack, that sort of thing. Finally, they sat in the pre-boarding lounge at the departure gate, and Helena learned a little about his life as a prizefighter, bouncer, and manager of a cattle ranch in Montana. Not her usual sort of beau, she thought, but oh, so attractive in a kind of hyper-masculine way.

"Were you on vacation in Las Vegas, Sam?" she asked.

"You could say that. But it was really part of my plan to make a new start. Not long ago an uncle of mine died and left me some money. It wouldn't be a great sum to most folks, but it's enough for me to spend time thinking about who I am and where I'm headed. I'd like to think I could find a management job in San Francisco."

"Good for you, Sam."

With his background, she wondered if that were really feasible, but he seemed aggressive and self-assured enough for ten managers. Who could say?

"One thing for sure. You're no gerbil," she said.

"Pardon?"

"Just an expression a woman in Las Vegas used. She's kind of a local legend, Wanda Buckley."

At the time it didn't faze her that he had no reply.

When they boarded, Sam took her overnight case right to her seat and tossed it in the overhead bin before heading back to first class. She noticed how shabby his carry-on bag looked. Men, she thought, so careless about some things. The guy is going first class with a piece of luggage that looks both old and cheap.

"See you in San Francisco, I hope."

"I hope so too, Sam."

She left it there. No use complicating her life.

Helena's seat was on the aisle. She felt the man next to her stare as she settled in. It wasn't long before he was chatting her up, but she found him hard to take. He was tall and thin and blond and boring. After ten minutes of parry and thrust with this jerk, she felt drained of energy. When the announcement came that passengers were free to move around the cabin, she was about to flee to the rest room.

But there was Sam Porter standing in the aisle, one hand on the seatback in front of her. His first words were directed at her seatmate.

33

"You know, we're quite good friends, Helena and I, and we'd really like to sit together. What do you say we change places? I'm in first class, it's very nice up there, and I've already told the flight attendant your drinks are on me."

Angela had to admire Sam's panache. He had a seductive smile, smooth delivery, and a persuasive manner. The blond fellow's jaw dropped. He looked from her to Sam, then bowed to the inevitable. At least he'd get a drink and some decent legroom out of the deal. He pulled his carry-on from under the seat in front of him and toddled off to first class.

"Sam," she said, "that man probably thinks we're lifelong friends. You are incorrigible."

"Well then, you'll have to *corrige* me, Helena. We've got the whole flight for it," he said while opening the overhead and pushing his bag in next to hers.

"M-m-m-m. I wonder, are you always so self-assured?"

"I suppose I can't help it. My take on things is that you have to know what you want out of life and be determined to get it. There's just no other way."

By now he had squeezed into the vacant seat, buckled in, and had turned to her with that grin of his. Helena couldn't think what to say to him. He was too forward, too cocky. She smiled and shook her head.

Their flight through the black velvet night sky was quiet and uneventful. The drone of the engines might have lulled Helena to sleep if she hadn't had to contend with Sam. After a while, she found herself stalling, deflecting personal questions with banter. She wanted to retain his interest without compromising herself. But with Sam's aggressive manner, keeping him under wraps for her private consumption wasn't going to be easy.

"What happened to your hand, Sam?" she asked.

The bandage wasn't terribly obtrusive, but she thought there must be a fairly substantial wound there.

"Just a clumsy accident with a knife. Couple of stitches took care of it. Listen, Helena, would you rather I stop asking questions? I realize we've just met, but I've told you a lot about myself, and I don't even know your full name."

"I don't mean to be coy, Sam. I'm just naturally . . . careful, I guess."

"You can't tell me even a little about yourself?"

"The thing is, I'm recently divorced. You might say I'm feeling vulnerable."

"Maybe you could tell me about your work in that case, or your family?"

She could sense he wasn't about to let it go, so she filled him in on Angela and the big influence in their lives, their father Sam Sharples. Their social status seemed to fascinate him, but for some reason she left out that she was adopted. Maybe she did it to give a better impression. Was she trying to reel him in? If she had wanted to push him away, she certainly could have. Truth be told, she had a yen for fun and games with Sam Porter in San Francisco, but without jeopardizing her relationship with Brad. She hadn't wanted to admit that to herself, but there it was.

~ ~ ~

Disembarking at the airport, they headed to the baggage claim. Helena had asked Angela not to meet her, told her she would engage a taxi for the ride home. She didn't want to see Brad right away, and Angela agreed to tell him that she spent the extra time in Las Vegas because the arrival of the divorce papers had depressed her. What she needed, of course, was a few hours breathing space. Brad would understand—nice men always understand when women react emotionally to something momentous like divorce.

Sam pulled their bags off the luggage carousel and waited while she asked a skycap to take hers to the ground transportation area.

"May I have your phone number, Helena?" he asked. "I'd like see you tomorrow."

"Oh, Sam, I have things that have to be taken care of tomorrow and the next day. Why don't you tell me where you'll be staying and I'll call you."

"I only decided to come to San Francisco this afternoon. I don't know yet where I'll be."

"You might like the Prado. It's near Market Street. Quite reasonable I've heard, but clean and safe."

"If you'll call, I promise to stay there," he said.

"I *will* call, Sam."

"Great. If you want a lift, I'm going to look for a rental now."

"No, Sam. That won't do. I'll find a taxi. I've inconvenienced you enough for one day."

He treated her to a full display of even white teeth. And the blue eyes sparkled.

"You're wrong, you know," he said. "I haven't had enough. Not nearly."

CHAPTER 7

NO MORE TRAILER PARK TRASH

LIEUTENANT VIEJO

IN HIS JOURNAL, Shoo-fly claims he was restless after checking into his room at the Prado. The place was a cut above decent, but he would have looked for cheaper left to his own devices. Helena's recommendation was his only reason for staying there.

He lit a cigarette and gazed out his window at the darkening street scene, feeling a kind of perturbation he hadn't known for a while. Helena Swann's face and form filled his mind. He had no doubt the attraction was mutual, but she had been wary, aloof at times. Was she playing her own game, he wondered, or would she help him? That was his bottom line. He needed somebody on his side, and she had the social and business connections that could ease the way.

So far, most of his life had been a series of missed chances, screw-ups because of his temper, frustration and anger that led to violence and crime. But he felt he'd paid his dues and was certain he could be as good or better than anybody with the right break. He stripped down to just a wife-beater and briefs and lay on the bed, reflecting on events from his past with a kind of passion to understand what made him this way.

In his mind's eye, he saw an image of himself as a boy on a Chicago city bus with his mother. They were dirt poor, his father a long gone drunk, his mother preoccupied and distant. Men came and went in her miserable life. He remembered how one, whom he had liked so much for the park visits and baseball games, took him on his lap one day and began to caress him in a way that made him sick. Later, that same man and his mother argued long and loud while he shed angry tears in his bed.

As a teenager, he left school and home behind and hitchhiked west. It wasn't always easy, but he felt free and strong. He fell in with a boxing promoter in Tucson and had a quick success as a young heavyweight. Shoo-fly bloodied any number of opponents but didn't much like getting hit himself. A broken nose was all it took to get him to stop. It wasn't the pain, and he wasn't afraid of anybody; he was simply tremendously vain about his appearance. He had the notion his looks could carry him a long way. With his savings from boxing, he took his time to find a better way to make a living. Over the next year, he took odd jobs and studied to earn a high school equivalency diploma.

Shoo-fly's jobs usually followed the same pattern. He'd be off to a great start, respected for his energy and cleverness . . . until something or someone blocked his way, driving him to a fit of temper. That was how he landed in jail. The charge was felonious assault with intent to kill, although the public defender got it plea-bargained down to simple assault.

He met Mickey in stir. The little guy was known for a mean shiv, but the big fellow was able to extend even more protection than his knife could. Shoo-fly had proved himself early on. One victorious prison-yard scuffle with a tough inmate was all it took for word to get around.

A program with the local junior college enabled Shoo-fly to earn an associate's degree in business administration while doing his time. He really got into it, following up by reading every self-help article and library book on business management he could get his hands on.

Mickey got out first, went to California and kept in touch. Six months later, it was Shoo-fly's turn. Upon release, he qualified for a state-funded program that resulted in a job at Blue Cross of Arizona. It looked like things were falling into place, but the program was terminated after nine months when funding ran out.

Mickey was quick to suggest coming out to the coast—and by then California sounded good to Shoo-fly. He spent a lot of time on the beach that summer in Venice. Jobs were scarce though, and he saw no future in the menial positions that satisfied his friend.

In Montana next, he went from ranch hand to foreman. He liked the life, could picture himself even now riding the fence line, bagging coyotes. Mickey tagged along with him, even after that bad scene with the hicks in the country bar. Shoo-fly had to get out of town then, which is how they wound up in Vegas.

The old, sad pattern of his had to change now, he saw that. He needed a better life—it was his time—and maybe Helena Swann would be the linchpin for his transformation. He was sure as hell gonna pursue it. He had big ideas, Shoo-fly did. And the business with Lana and Randy? Forget that—it would never happen again. No more trailer park trash for Shoo-fly.

The next day, he steeled himself for his assault on San Francisco. He got up early and thought everything over carefully at breakfast. Then he marked time until late afternoon, taking a long stroll through the city. Back at the hotel, he put on fresh clothes, grabbed his hat, and checked himself out in the dresser mirror before leaving.

Helena thought he had no idea where she lived. But he knew she lived with her sister, and it was her sister's name and address he had seen on the luggage tags in the baggage claim at San Francisco airport.

Shoo-fly hadn't forgotten that address.

CHAPTER 8

A FUNNY OLD BAG

WHEN THE MURDERS at Wanda Buckley's occurred, Pedro Brunetti had been an investigator in Las Vegas for thirteen years. P.I.'s are often retired cops, but he fell into it after some years in security with the gaming industry. When a guy starts from that perspective, he's already seen a lot of grifters. He knows how to spot guys and gals on the make, and he develops a feel for what they'll do, how they'll react, where to find them. As a P.I. in Vegas, you don't do many divorces like you would elsewhere. Las Vegas just marries 'em and sends them back to your fair city for the divorce action a year or two down the road.

Like everyone else in town, Pedro knew Wanda Buckley. She called him not long after the headlines popped with the gory details about Lana Firewood and Randy Prinz, and the mystery surrounding their slaughter. But what ground could he cover when the whole of the Las Vegas police force was out scouring every bar, casino and hotel for information? He commiserated with her on the loss of her friend, and asked her what she thought he might do for her.

"Pedro," she said, "Lana was a swell person and I'm gonna make it my life's mission, so help me, to bag the sonuvabitch who did this."

"But Wanda, my dove, the police are certainly on it, and they have the resources for this sort of thing. They won't be sharing details with me, regardless of your standing in the case."

"I love the way you talk, Pedro. I didn't even know I had 'standing.' But just listen up a minute. I keep telling

41

those cops to find the new boyfriend, the one Lana talked about lately. She even said he was the jealous type."

"You've given his name to the police, Wanda?"

"Aw, I don't know it. He had a casino job, but it's not as if I ever met him."

"Description, Wanda?"

"Big fella, she told me. Nice dresser."

"M-m-m-m. Big, huh? Works in a casino. Not a lot to go on, my friend."

"I know Pedro, I know. But I want somebody on this full time. The cops just look at me when I talk about the boyfriend. Like maybe he's real and maybe he isn't. Pedro, I *know* it's him!"

"Okay, Wanda, okay. If you're sure you want a full-time investigation, I'll do it. But this could be a long haul."

They talked retainer, and she got her first shock when Pedro told her it would be two thousand to start and he'd be back for more when he'd used up fifty hours. But he knew she had the money—and to spare—with the way the real estate business had been booming for years in the valley. Wanda may have struck folks as a funny old bag, but she was rich as Croesus.

"Can you find him, Pedro? That's all I care about now."

"Well Wanda, like it says in Numbers, *'Be sure that your sin will find you out.'* What I've got to do is facilitate that."

CHAPTER 9

BODIES IN THE KITCHEN

HOME FOR HELENA in San Francisco was her sister's mansion in the Marina district. She had moved back in after her separation from Jeremy. Even though Angela was at pains to make sure Helena understood it was her home too, that was a polite fiction. The place was in Angela's name alone.

The morning after her flight from Las Vegas, Helena showered and dressed early, then joined her sister on the terrace where the housekeeper was serving breakfast. They sat and ate, not saying much. Angela kept gazing out toward the bay, and Helena got the idea she was avoiding eye contact.

"Is something wrong?" she asked, trying to make her voice sound deferential.

"I don't want to seem a scold, Helena, but I didn't like lying to Brad yesterday. Telling him you were upset about the divorce papers and not telling him what really kept you in Las Vegas didn't sit right with me."

Helena covered her face with both hands.

"You're being kind," she whispered. "Not only did I ask you to lie, I had you making phone calls about bodies in the kitchen. I'm sorry, Angela. I was in a terrible bind and couldn't see another way out. Bear with me through this and I'll try to be better."

"Brad will be over this afternoon. Be better for *him*, honey. He deserves it."

She was right about that. But didn't Helena deserve better after what she'd been through? Angela's life was a magical money show; she was so sheltered she didn't have to recognize any deviation from the straight and narrow. That was for lesser folk.

But it wouldn't be wise to contradict her, so Helena held her tongue. Angela was very generous to her after all, would never refuse a request for help, never stint in supporting her lifestyle. And Helena loved her sister, even as she wanted a life lived away from the lovely chains that bound them together.

"By the way, Helena, I didn't see anything in the morning paper about . . . a murder in Las Vegas."

"Thank God!" she said. "What did Wanda Buckley say when you called her?"

"I didn't give her time to say anything. My voice was shaking, and I had barely gotten out the words when I just hung up and came back home."

Now Helena really did feel bad. It had been a rotten trick to involve her sister. She stood up, came quickly around to Angela's side of the table, and put her arms around her from behind. The bay breeze that wafted over them was fresh and sweet.

Angela looked up smiling and patted her hands

"Helena?" she asked.

"What, dear?"

"A minute ago you said *bodies* in the kitchen. What did you mean? I thought there was one body."

"That's right. I saw just one. I only meant I had you calling people about *bodies* . . . in a general sense. You know?"

"Yes. I see."

~ ~ ~

The morning papers may have had nothing about the gore fest at Wanda Buckley's, but the cable news channels were full of it by early afternoon. They didn't give out all the details Helena had seen, but it was sensational nonetheless, and Mrs. Buckley's florid face was shown over and over, bemoaning the death of her good friend Lana Firewood. Helena pretended to be shocked by the second murder of the 'as-yet-unidentified' young man, and she was relieved when Angela didn't pick up again on that slip she had made about 'bodies' in the kitchen.

They were glued to Fox News when Brad dropped in. Helena raced out to him when she heard the housekeeper tell him they were in the library.

"Hi, Baby!" He opened his arms wide when he saw her. "You're looking incredible today."

They kissed and strolled out to the terrace, arm in arm. Angela was beaming, having come out of the library to meet them.

"I'll leave you two alone now. Nice to see you Brad."

"No, Angela, stay! Unless, of course, you can't stand the sight of us pawing each other after a week apart."

"Wouldn't exactly be the first time I've been treated to that, my friend. You go right ahead and I'll just blush modestly over here by the potted palm."

Everything is perfect now, Helena thought, three beautiful people on the terrace of a mansion in San Francisco. Joking, laughing, sharing affection and pleasant conversation. There wasn't a single cloud on the horizon—neither in the blue sky nor in her future. Brad looked handsome in his pink polo shirt and Dockers; Angela was blonde and slim, lovely and tan against her white shorts and pale green cashmere sweater. Just to look at them made her feel happy and secure. Esther, the housekeeper, brought a tray of drinks to them on the terrace. Life was grand.

Early that evening, the doorbell rang while the three of them were chatting in the living room. When Esther came in to announce a Mister Porter, Sam was right behind her, soft hat in hand. Helena had no idea how to cover this, so she just stood up and started talking, very much aware of the two expectant faces of Brad and Angela.

"Why, hello Sam. Good to see you," she said. "Sam Porter, I'd like you to meet Angela Sharples, my sister. And this is Brad Styles, my fiancé."

Now it was Sam's turn to cover. She held her breath for what would come next.

"How do, pleased to meet you both," he said.

Brad had stood up. Sam advanced and shook hands with him.

"I'm sorry to barge in like this," he said. "Helena and I sat together on the flight from Las Vegas last night. She spoke a lot about her dad . . . and yours, Miss Sharples. He was an authentic legend and I admired him very much. I have some ideas for the communications industry you folks are involved with, and I thought I might catch Helena alone to discuss them. But it's obviously the wrong time. Maybe I can call on you another day, Helena."

Irritated by his presumption to show up like this, she was nevertheless impressed with his performance. He's a little rough around the edges at times, she thought, but he came through with a plausible story. Still, she wanted to take him up on his offer to leave.

"All right, Sam," she said. "Why don't you give me your phone number? One of us will get back to you tomorrow."

Angela piped up at this. "Actually, we were about to go to Bidouri, a little club not far from here, Mr. Porter," she said. "Care to go with us?"

"Oh Angela," Helena cut in, trying to derail the idea. "I'm sure Sam has things to do his first full day in San Francisco."

"Well, no," he said. "I have no plans at all after this call. I'd love to join your party."

He looked at Helena a trifle defiantly as he said it, then directed a charming smile at Angela.

"I can't tell you how glad I am you can come,"

Angela said. "Otherwise, I was going to be the extra woman—*de trop*, as the French say. You're saving me from that, Mr. Porter."

"My pleasure, Angela. And call me Sam, please."

Angela wasn't the type of person to look for payback, but she was certainly making up for any ill use Helena had subjected her to yesterday. And Sam Porter was looking at her the way he had when she bet against his dice toss in Las Vegas.

"Good, that's settled," she said, trying hard for a jovial note. But the whole situation stuck deep in her craw. Sam was going to be a handful to manage.

They took Brad's Escalade to the club. He was quiet on the short trip over while Sam was full of questions and Angela only too eager to give him pointers about things to do and see in San Francisco.

By the time they were settled at a table in Bidouri, Helena was afraid Brad would be looking to her for answers about Sam. Angela got her off the hook temporarily by asking if she might dance with Brad. The combo at the bandstand was playing a bluesy version of *I Wish You Love*—the tenor sax starting a long solo.

"Well, Brad does like the slow ones for dancing. Go ahead darling, but save the next one for me."

"Okay, Miss Sharples, you're on," Brad laughed. "It's good to know someone finds my charms irresistible."

After watching them mix in with the other couples on the dance floor, Sam and Helena turned to each other with uneasy looks.

"You really should have told me you have a fiancé," he said.

"I suppose, and you really should have told me you intended to visit. May I ask how you found out where I live?"

"Luggage tags. Is he rich, your guy?"

"Very."

"How soon do you plan to marry?"

"Brad's mother is ill. As soon as she's well enough to attend the wedding."

"I'll bet I could make you change your mind about marrying Mr. Brad."

"What incredible egotism! What in the world makes you think you could accomplish that miracle?"

"Oh, I don't think it would take a miracle. You and I have a certain chemistry, Helena, and I know you feel it the same way I do. When I go after something I really want, I'm willing to do what it takes."

"Let's get something straight, Mr. Porter. What we may or may not have is quite beside the point. My relationship with Brad is important to me. He stands for stability and security. I need that and I don't intend to mess up."

"I get it. You're considering me for a playmate as long as there's no real danger of losing your meal ticket."

"Look, I find your manner unbearable. If you want to fence with me, fine. But if you think alienating me is going to advance your cause, think twice, Sam."

He looked at her steadily and nodded. She judged him contrite but unbowed.

"Let me apologize, Helena. I had no right to say those things. But you've got to make allowances for me. You gave me no idea that I hadn't a chance with you."

He was right about that. She had toyed with him, and he found her out. For a minute, they were silent, turning their attention again to the dance floor. When the band segued to an up-tempo song, Brad came back to the table with Angela trailing.

"Sam, dance with me, please," Angela asked. "Papa Brad is too old for this sort of thing."

"Papa Brad, indeed. I simply want to hold on to my

dignity."

Helena laughed. "Sit right here, Papa, and I'll hold on to it with you."

Brad was in a good mood now, and the questions he had for Helena didn't amount to much. He only wondered why Sam had the impression that Helena was part of the communications industry, as were he and Angela. She told him they had talked about the newspaper and cable channel, and that Sam must have made an assumption, probably because she was conversant with the issues.

Brad's back was to the dance floor while Helena faced out to it. As they held hands and chatted, she kept an eye on Sam and Angela. That bastard was making time with her sister. Through fast and slow numbers, he pressed close to her, eyes fixed on hers, smiling and saying things that seemed to both enchant her and keep her off balance.

But Helena had Brad and nothing else should matter. She told herself she was worried about Angela and that ravenous wolf. Whether or not she convinced herself was another question.

"Interesting guy, Sam," said Brad. "I think I'll ask him to drop by my office and tell me about those ideas of his."

Oh great, she thought, maybe you'll hire him and Angela will marry him. Where the hell was this going?

CHAPTER 10

THE FAT PAL

A FEW DAYS AFTER SAM went off his nut at Wanda Buckley's place, a cop came around to the bar where Mickey Cullion worked. Mickey figured this was what you would call inevitable. They were hitting every dive in town; so he knew Sparky's, a dive for sure, would not be an exception. The cop's name was Janeway, Detective Martin Janeway. Looked to Mickey like he had his shield maybe two weeks. Before even question one, he knew how this would go.

Yes, officer, I read the newspaper . . . . No, I don't remember anybody or anything suspicious around that time . . . . Do I know a big guy works in a casino? Well, yeah, maybe a hundred or so. Ha, ha . . . . What's that, anybody I know left town around that time? Well, shoot, a buddy of mine left for home around then—family trouble. Yeah, he's a big guy . . . . Name? Sam Porter's the name I knew him by—I guess it could be an alias, couldn't really say . . . . Worked at a casino like everybody else—the Riviera, I'm pretty sure. . . . No, I'm not in touch with him, wouldn't expect to see him again, to tell you the truth . . . . Sure, I'll let you know.

Questions asked and answered, Janeway gave Mickey his card and that was that. Only thing really bothered him was the cop's pal hanging around in the background while Mickey polished glasses and the cop asked his questions. Ever notice a bartender starts polishing glasses when he's got nothing to do but don't want it to show? Anyway, Mickey knew the cop's fat pal from somewhere, and he was pretty sure he wasn't no cop.

So, Sam's name was out there. Like a hundred others, no doubt. Mickey kept as close to the truth as possible because a smart con either doesn't know or says something he can stick to. He had to mention Sam because the police could already have some information. A lie about that could be dangerous. If he came back with more questions, it might be time to run, but not yet. Mickey didn't volunteer that Sam lived with him—then again, he hadn't been asked. He was okay so far.

Sam's first call from Frisco came later that day. Mickey told him what happened, which ticked Sam off, but he tried to make him see he'd done what he had to. Sam didn't say where he was staying and Mickey didn't ask.

"This cop had a buddy with him, Sam. Some guy I seen around, but I can't figure where."

"So what? They always come in pairs, like vultures."

"No, the fat boy wasn't no cop."

They went over what Mickey knew about the investigation, how it had stalled as far as he could tell. The medical examiner was having a press conference tomorrow, and he'd go hear what he had to say. And then Sam dropped the bomb.

"I'm tight with a gal here, Mickey. Rich as sin and big time connections."

"Good luck with that, pal."

"We're going to get married."

"Whoa! Who the hell is she?"

"All I'm gonna say right now, Mick, is that she's in the big leagues."

"Jesus, Sam. When is this gonna come off?"

"I don't know. I haven't asked her yet."

Nothing about Sam could surprise him by this time, but that was news he would have to chew over. Jealous? Well, maybe. Before he hung up, Sam said he had a bead on a good job and there might be something in it for Mickey. He was supposed to be ready to come to San Francisco on short notice.

"When you leave Vegas, Mick, you won't be letting anybody know."

"Got it, Sam. Just move on like always, without a trace."

"Such a smart kid."

"Learned from the masters. No sense starting over if your past can catch up with you and bite you in the ass."

CHAPTER 11

ASSAULT ON SAN FRANCISCO

WITHOUT HESITATION, Sam Porter took Brad Styles up on his offer to drop by. At first, the whole thing seemed a bit of a lark, but when Sam left his office after their meeting, Brad had to admit that first impressions and outward appearances can be *totally* deceiving. Underneath Sam's rough and ready manner were a penetrating intelligence and a wealth of management ideas for Sharples Communications.

The guy knocked him out. He had no visual aids, no PowerPoint presentation, and no notes of any kind. The vision he laid out would shake up Sharples' hidebound management structure and was totally committed to increasing the newspaper's circulation. Sam called their cable channel TNT lite, an assessment that put Brad's problems with that venture in a new perspective.

Unlike some communications conglomerates, Sharples had never embraced a product management approach to news and entertainment. Sam saw them adding product teams under the managing editors and senior journalists. The whole idea was meant to break down the newspaper's sections, like Arts & Entertainment, into products that could be tied to customer segments. From there, research would tell management what these segments really wanted to find on their doorsteps every day. Although the new positions would require specialized knowledge, he thought Brad could avoid establishing a new level of management by challenging the responsible editors to take charge of product management goals.

Sam also believed that the senior journalists and

columnists should be required to adopt a "publish or perish" philosophy on the pattern of university professors. Editorial management could form an agency to represent them and their books—or Sharples might even revive the publishing house that had been started and dropped years ago. With this idea, the company's best talent would become brands suitable for promotion. Sharples would be adopting a posture that could lead to more writing and journalism awards than ever before. Besides all this, Sam had excellent product development and brand management ideas for the cable channel, although he hadn't had time to develop them in detail.

Brad was nearly in shock. He thought he had invited the guy to meet as a favor to Helena, and maybe to amuse himself a little. Instead, he ended by offering him a consulting job.

When Brad turned the conversation around to more personal matters at lunch, Sam was very forthcoming that this would be his first substantial position in the business world. Before this, he had only filled a product manager position at a Blue Cross plan after college. Brad had never heard of his school, but that didn't concern him much. His only job managing people was that ranch foreman position he told Helena about. Even that didn't matter to Brad. He thought he recognized a dynamic, results-oriented performer when he saw one.

Over the next couple of weeks, they would need to work out a budget for the project, and Brad would introduce him to all the line management people he had to work with. Today, the directive he gave Sam was to have the concept up and running in six months with buy-in from all the managing editors and senior journalists. He was elated to be in charge of a major project at a prestigious company and had only one concern.

"I want to be clear about my chain of command, Brad. I realize you're up at the executive level, and I'll work for whoever you want, but I would certainly prefer to report to you. At least during the conceptual phase of the project."

"I was thinking you might fit best with the senior managing editor. But I suppose that could slow us down at first. Tell you what . . . to get this moving fast, you *will* report directly to me. Just don't let me hear of any friction between you and staff. I'll lay down the law that this project is priority number one for us."

"Thanks, Brad," he said. "Thanks for this chance. You won't regret it."

Finally, he told Sam to report to Human Resources and fill out the necessary forms for payroll authorization. He would also need to supply references and his curriculum vitae as soon as that was convenient. Putting the thought aside that he was taking a risk, Brad assured himself that a failure to grab hold of a genuine talent like Sam would be a sin of omission, a signal failure on his part.

When Sam stopped by later to request an advance, Brad authorized it for him.

CHAPTER 12

THE HUGE PLAY

THAT EVENING HELENA SWANN sat in her room, trying to get the jumbled thoughts of Brad, her divorce, and those murders in Las Vegas out of her mind for a moment. Too much had happened too quickly for her to process. Adding to her confusion was Sam Porter's pursuit of her sister. There was an undercurrent of danger in everything that man did.

She had pretended indifference when Angela went with him to dinner, but she was troubled. Although her proper focus just now was staying close to Brad, she felt a twinge of responsibility for Angela's welfare. Or was it jealousy? Towards midnight, Angela burst into her room. She must have seen the light under the door.

Angela's radiant look was a giveaway. Anybody could see she was falling in love. Should Helena try to intervene? More than anyone, she knew how vulnerable Angela was after a life of being sheltered from everything that wasn't best for her. Their dynamic father Sam Sharples was a very protective parent who set the male ideal for both of them. Then there were the right schools and the best social life money could buy.

Helena, too, had shared these things, but there was a difference between them that often rankled—the knowledge that Angela was the real daughter, the natural child, the fairy princess everyone loved. She had a regal bearing, a sweet temperament and a manner that kept the rough and tumble elements of everyday life at arm's length. A friend once remarked that Angela never *attended* a social gathering, she *presided* over it.

That was Angela, all right.

"How do you know you're in love, Helena?" she asked. "When did you first realize you loved Brad?"

Helena slumped in her chair and raised an eyebrow.

"Pardon me for thinking this is not about Brad and me," she said. "Why don't we talk about what you're feeling? Tell me about your dinner with Sam. Seems to me your newest employee made quite an impression. Or . . . was it a conquest?"

"Don't make fun of me, Helena. Not tonight. I suppose it's obvious I have strong feelings for him. No man has had this kind of effect on me before. Tell me what to expect."

"I'm beginning to think *you* should tell *me* what to expect! Oh, honey, I think you're in for quite a ride. Nobody can tell you what you should do or how you should feel. I do have one piece of advice, though. Enjoy yourself, but be careful. Tell him to slow down whenever you feel the least bit pressured or uncomfortable."

So there it was. Sam was making a huge play for Angela, and she was out in the cold. Helena could hardly blame him, but lovely, sweet, warm Angela was not his kind of woman. Who the hell was he kidding? And what was she going to do about it?

~ ~ ~

The Prado is neither the best nor the worst small hotel in San Francisco. Before settling in with Angela in the Marina district, Helena had stayed there a week when she moved out of the house near Big Sur that she and Jeremy had been renting. Although much of the hotel's business is transient, the management prefers customers looking to secure a short-term lease, such as young professionals new to the city.

Sam was on the third floor of this little establishment. Helena went to see him without calling first. As a pretext for her outing, she informed Esther she would be in the city shopping all afternoon. Not knowing whether Sam would be in, she walked into the lobby and spoke to the desk clerk. Put off somehow by his snobbish little face, she decided to try an official tone.

"Sam Porter is an acquaintance of mine and an employee of my fiancé," she said. "Would you please let him know I'm here? My name is Helena Swann. I'll wait just over here while you call him."

She sat in an upholstered armchair about ten feet away from the counter. She hadn't let the desk clerk ask any questions and wasn't looking at him now, but heard him pick up an extension and speak to someone for a few moments.

"Ms. Swann?" he called out, a little too loudly. "Mr. Porter requests that you see him in his room. It's 307. The elevator is to my left, just around the corner of the lobby."

She didn't say thank you, merely dropped the newspaper she had picked up and walked off to find the elevator. The little shit's voice had dripped with sarcasm. And she was furious that Sam hadn't the decency to come down to the lobby and receive her properly.

By the time she knocked at his door, Helena had forced herself to calm down. If she called him to account, he would only laugh at her for standing on ceremony.

"Helena," he said, opening the door with a grin and a flash of blue eyes. "Helena Troia, the face that launched a thousand ships."

"Clever," she laughed. "And this must be Sam the stupendous, the man who conquered San Francisco."

"Well, I warned you I'd try," he said as she walked in.

The room had that banal troika of hotel décor, the chair-table-chair by the window, where they sat facing each other.

"Sam, I'm amazed. You were as good as your word. You know, Brad prides himself on being a terrific judge of character. In your case, I'm not so sure, but I want you to know he's a great guy all around, and I expect you to be the kind of employee he deserves."

"Ah, the things you expect, Helena."

"I'll tell you what I haven't been expecting. The big rush on Angela."

"She's a beautiful girl."

"And a good one, a very good one. Don't hurt her, Sam."

"Helena, you seem to have low expectations as far I'm concerned. Where are your manners?"

"*My* manners! Why you presumptuous fake. Where were your manners when you told that piddling desk clerk to have me come up here like some piece of trash off the street?"

She was fuming, but she backed off. "Now I'm sorry I said that."

"Don't be. You're right, I'm just a guy from nowhere on the make. But I want to be somebody, and you can help. You could teach me a lot of things I need to know."

She stood up. "Somehow I can't imagine you could learn a whole lot from me. I think it was a mistake, my coming here."

He got up quickly and moved toward her with a long, hard sigh. Before she could react, his arms had enveloped her and his lips were hot against hers. The muscular frame pressing close, the eager tongue probing—this was what she had hoped for and what she was afraid of. Her emotions may have been in conflict, but her body responded to him at once.

He made love in the same straightforward way he did everything. It was passionate, brutal at times, but with an animal grace that left Helena panting for more. At every stage of their lovemaking, he made sure that her needs were being met, then tried to surpass them. She stayed with him for three hours, until it wasn't safe to stay any longer. While she dressed to go, he watched from the bed, naked, smiling that insolent smile. Neither of them spoke as she leaned over and kissed him one last time before walking out the door.

CHAPTER 13

A CERTAIN ARROGANCE

ANGELA WOULD ALWAYS remember their first meetings at the little nightclub and at dinner the very next day. Sam had taken her by storm. There was something in his manner so forthright and unrelenting that she couldn't quite get her bearings. Except for her father, no man in her life had ever been—masterful like Sam.

Later on, she would analyze the similarities between them—her new Sam and her dad Sam Sharples. Good looks, charm, dynamism, pride, and yes—a certain arrogance and ruthlessness. But her father was a respected and productive citizen after a tumultuous youth. Why couldn't Sam Porter follow that same path? Wasn't it obvious there was something . . . extraordinary about him?

Helena accused her of falling fast, but even she didn't know how completely. Angela's love for Sam was total, committed, desperate. She thought she had found a father, friend and lover all wrapped up in one gorgeous package. He was so unlike the *safe* boys in their set that she was enchanted, and yet she would never have thought he was *unsafe*, or unscrupulous or unbalanced. Still, with her limited experience, how could she tell?

Her first dance with him in the club set a pattern. The number was jazzy, up-tempo, and she was afraid she couldn't follow his lead well enough. Her first words to him were, "Sam, you're too close."

"I can't help it," he said. "When I look at you, I see everything a man could want and more. You're beautiful, warm and gracious. You'll have to pardon me, Angela. I'll try to maintain some distance, but it won't be easy."

"Now look, if you're trying to make me blush, you're doing a good job," she laughed. "You're really way too forward!"

"Look, Angela, I can't be the first guy to get carried away like this. Certainly *all* the men you know aren't immune to beauty and grace."

"Sam, please. What makes you think I've even been noticed in this town?"

"Shame on San Francisco if you haven't!"

By the time he asked if she were free for dinner the next day, Angela couldn't have said no if she tried. Back at the table with Helena and Brad, she noticed something distant in her sister's interaction with Sam, which surprised her. After all, she was the one he had initially called on. Brad, on the other hand, seemed to like his brashness and even asked him to come around and talk about his business ideas. Brad's subsequent hiring of him was a kind of validation of Angela's high opinion.

The weeks that followed were a whirlwind for her. Sam came out to the house nearly every day after work. On weekends, they did the simple things around San Francisco that newcomers do, getting acquainted with the city. There were strolls around North Beach and Fisherman's Wharf, trips to Telegraph Hill and Coit tower to look at the murals, dozens of little touristy things that she enjoyed for his sake. Sam had tremendous energy and could walk forever. He had a tendency to want to explore more than Angela did, areas like the Mission district that she had been taught to steer clear of.

She stored up these memories of her and Sam with great fondness. Fondness, she thought, for the good in him. Later on, everyone would talk as if he were pure evil, but she knew better. At least, she had to believe she did.

When Sam asked her to marry him, Angela was so flustered, she wept. Her hands flew to her face as she felt the hot tears sting her cheeks.

"Angela, baby, the last thing I wanted to do was make you cry," he laughed.

When she could look up at him, his brilliant smile was reassuring—but his eyes were insistent.

"Say yes, darling," he said.

"Yes, darling."

It was Angela's turn to laugh. She wiped away the tears and threw her arms around those broad shoulders. Happiness had overtaken her, and her equanimity had fled. She wanted to run through the streets and proclaim her devotion.

That night wasn't the first time they made love, but it was very special to her. They had never been to his room in the Prado previously. That was one thing she would not do before this. Even for Sam.

"You know you're the first woman ever to set foot in my room, Angela."

"Well, I had better be, Sam Porter!" she said.

CHAPTER 14

LEAVE THE KNIFE AT HOME

JANEWAY'S FAT PAL turned out to be Pedro Brunetti, a P.I. who used to work for the casinos. He came up to Mickey Cullion after the medical examiner's press conference and made like they were old friends. The M.E. had given his official opinion that the deaths of Lana and Randy were the result of multiple puncture wounds, just like everybody knew he would.

"How's it going?" Brunetti said. "What brings you around?"

"I got the morning off, was walkin' around and saw the crowd outside, so I stopped by," Mickey said. "You got something to do with this?"

"No, not really. I have a private ticket, just covering some bases for a friend who knew one of the victims."

"I thought you were working on it with that cop, what's his face."

"See, he's a buddy. I just tagged along that day to get a feel for the case. You know, he found out later both victims got around to a lot of the bars."

"Never asked me about that."

"That's why I came over. You told him you read the newspaper stories, so you've seen their names and pictures. Ever see them at your place?"

"At Sparky's? No, never. I could've seen them other places, because I get around too, but I'd remember if they ever came in my place."

"Does that mean you *have* seen them someplace?"

"Nah, not that I remember. Just means I could've, you know?"

Brunetti seemed to lose interest after that and

drifted off. But Mickey was glad they talked. It came to him that Brunetti was the private dick who tracked down a buddy of his behind in his child support payments. The fat man wouldn't remember Mickey from that case, and now Mickey could forget about him.

The cops never followed up with more questions about Sam—and the newspaper stories had dwindled down to half a column now and then on some back page. That investigation was so dead, sometimes he didn't even bother to go through the morning paper until late at night. Not long after the M.E.'s press conference, Sam called from a pay phone in San Francisco to the house phone at the motel. You could tell things were going good for him by the edge in his voice.

"I'm close to the gold, Mickey, real close. Things are breaking my way for once."

"Hey, good for you."

"When you get here, you'll see what I mean. And there's a job in it for you, kid. You'll be like a messenger, a gofer at nine bucks an hour. You'll need to behave, leave the knife at home, but I guarantee you're gonna like it."

Mickey figured he could be right, but he wouldn't be leaving the shiv at home for nobody, not even good buddy Sam—who had an update for him on the girl he wanted to marry.

"She said yes," he said. "I already bought a tux." *If he's getting married,* Mickey thought, *how come he wants me around?*

If he's getting married, Mickey thought, how come he wants me around? He could pull any kid off the street for the messenger job. It didn't impress him that they were old friends. Sam wasn't the sentimental type.

They say you're supposed to keep your friends close but your enemies closer. Since Mickey was the only one who knew what happened in Vegas, it seemed to him he'd better figure out which of those two categories he fell into

~ ~ ~

Everybody traveling from Las Vegas to San Francisco catches a flight from McCarran. Not Mickey, though. Sam had sent him a little dough to get started, and he figured to save some of it by taking the bus in. He had one big suitcase, the soft-side type, which he got second hand at the Salvation Army, and he packed it tight. In fact, he had to unzip the expandable part to get everything in. And this was after cleaning out the motel room and throwing everything away but the bare essentials. All the porno magazines, even the Las Vegas mementos had to go. The porn didn't matter to him anyway; it was all Sam's girlie stuff.

He slept through the bus ride into town. It was mid-morning. After ditching the suitcase in a locker, he knocked around the city for a while. He hadn't been there for a long time and couldn't say it had changed much. People tell you how much they love the place, but it didn't amount to much in Mickey's opinion.

To him, it was a lifeless town, trading on some old memories that weren't so great to begin with. North Beach and Fisherman's Wharf had no color or pizzazz, unless you thought postcards, trinkets and rip-off strip shows are where it's at. Downtown was better, but not what you would call spectacular.

Anyway, that's how Mickey saw it. Sometimes, he got into arguments about it from people towing the party line that this fog-bound burg was the great American city. The fuckin' hills are murder if you're on foot, he thought. Give me L.A. or Vegas any day. He did like the cable cars, though.

He found a place to stay in the Mission district, not so far from where Sam was downtown at the Prado. The landlord gave him a deal for a little efficiency apartment with a bath and a kind of kitchenette. After he paid the first two weeks rent, he retrieved his bag from the locker and settled in. He was kind of proud of himself. He had made a nice clean break from Las Vegas.

CHAPTER 15

IF PAY PHONES COULD TALK

NOW THAT PEDRO BRUNETTI was on Wanda Buckley's dime, he didn't plan to get off, but she wasn't going to pay for zero results indefinitely. She'd want to know what leads he had, who he was investigating. Sad to say, what Pedro had so far would not impress her.

It didn't sit right with him that Mickey Cullion was at that press conference, and he wasn't sure he told the truth about not knowing Lana or Randy. But there was nowhere to go with it. Still, Pedro had a feeling. The only real clue was the call from San Francisco warning Wanda something was wrong at home. Telephone records showed that it came from a pay phone.

If only pay phones could talk, he thought.

Then the little weasel disappeared without a trace. Pedro managed to get into Mickey's motel room, but it was clean. He learned he had shared the place with Sam Porter, the friend he said took off for home. When he nosed around about the two men, he found out that Porter was a casino dealer, popular with the ladies. Cullion was a quiet little guy who palled around with Porter, but kept to himself otherwise.

Pedro knew he'd have nothing until he could convince the cops to take a look at this Porter. And that was not about to happen this century. Janeway wasn't ready to subpoena personnel records from the Riviera, or anyplace else for that matter. There were too many names of transients who left Las Vegas around that time. Porter was not a priority as far as the Las Vegas police were concerned.

It occurred to him that San Francisco might be

where both of them had gone. After all, some lady was there who made a certain phone call. Maybe his two bozos knew something and were looking for her. He'd just have to convince his client to let him track them down. She was at home when he called.

"Wanda, my sweet, I need to go to San Francisco to follow up a hunch I have."

"A hunch. I'm paying for hunches? What do you take me for? I want proof, Pedro!"

"Of course you do, dear, *Where your treasure is, there will your heart be also.* Now please listen, I think our answer is in San Francisco. That phone call you got came from a woman there. And I'd like to know more about two people who have left town. Where did they go? But if you wish to end the investigation, you would receive a small rebate for unused hours."

He was pretty sure that would stifle the old bitch.

"Pedro, I want you to find the boyfriend and you know it. Is one of these grifters the boyfriend?"

"Unfortunately, only poor Lana could have told you. More to the point, Wanda, somebody in San Francisco has a guilty conscience. Not the animal who murdered your friend, but somebody who knows something. Maybe a witness, I don't know."

~ ~ ~

Perhaps that pay phone could talk, after all. Wanda's telephone company pinpointed its exact location for him. He took an early morning flight to San Francisco and found it downtown in the lobby of the Tremont Building. When he looked at the office directory, there were only a few tenants. The major one by far was Sharples Communications, taking up several floors. It might be a long shot, but what if someone who worked in the building made that phone call?

Sharples Communications turned out to be the publisher of the San Francisco Record, the town's third largest newspaper. The president was Angela Sharples, the executive director Bradford Styles. Pedro thought that was swell, but where could he go with it? Even if a big shot consented to give him the time of day, how would he elicit his or her cooperation?

Another way of ferreting out information might be the reporters who worked there. They would probably frequent a favorite bar, wouldn't they? Would the name Sam Porter ring a bell with anyone? Mickey Cullion would have just arrived in San Francisco, so no one would know him yet.

Hoping the pay phone would bring him luck, Pedro used it to call Sharples Communications and asked for Mr. Bradford Styles. He reached an assistant, a young woman who asked his business.

"It's a personal matter concerning your company and an event that took place some weeks ago in Las Vegas."

Would that ring a bell with Bradford Styles? Damned if he knew.

Styles came to the phone after a few minutes.

"Mr. Brunetti, I can't think what you could possibly be talking about."

If that were really the case, why didn't you have your assistant brush me off, he wondered. Instead of probing for more information, he decided to back and fill, said he was sorry to bother him, that his information must have been faulty.

"But what was the personal matter, and what event in Las Vegas are we talking about?"

Pedro didn't tell him. Styles was just too pointedly curious. Something was bothering the man, something Pedro didn't know how to exploit. If Styles were curious enough, he could look him up in Las Vegas, where he would find a telephone number and an answering service. When Pedro checked for messages later, he'd be interested in seeing if anyone from Sharples Communications wanted to talk.

Before the end of his first day in San Francisco, he learned that the other top executive, Angela Sharples, was a multimillionaire heiress with a mansion in the Marina district. Everyone in town seemed to know her name. Beautiful young woman, noted socialite. Man oh man, what was he getting into?

Pedro felt as if he were on a leaky boat fishing in deep water. He might snag something that was too big or make a wrong move. In either case, he could find himself sinking fast, with no possibility of rescue. He decided to leave the big fish alone for now and find out where reporters for the San Francisco Record hung out.

CHAPTER 16

TWO GOOD SCRIPTS

THE WEDDING TOOK PLACE at home. Simple, elegant: for family and close friends only. Helena Swann had planned it down to the smallest detail. But it was *Angela's* wedding, not hers. This was intolerable to her, but she had to swallow it, smile and be happy for her dear sister and new brother-in-law. It would be their day, after all. Everyone had assumed Helena's marriage to Brad would come long before the fairy princess tied the knot for the first time, but Sam had turned their perfect, predictable little world upside down.

And now her relationship with Brad had taken a disquieting turn. All of a sudden, he was suspicious about everything: Sam (whom she had been careful to stay away from lately), her vacation in Las Vegas, and the little fellow Sam hired as messenger boy. This Mickey person was someone Helena didn't have a clue about. At first, she thought Brad's mother's illness was behind his sullen new mood, but when she expressed alarm, his reaction was sharp.

"Helena, at this late date your interest in my mother seems a stretch. Still, I've never held it against you that you don't get along with her. I know she can be difficult."

"That hurts, Brad. I don't know what to say, except that my interest is you and your feelings and whatever touches you. I know something's wrong. If it's anything I've done, let me make it right."

"What do you know about Sam Porter?" he asked.

"What do *I* know? Brad, Sam is your employee. I

only shared a flight with him from Las Vegas."

"Something about Las Vegas has me on edge," he said. "You, Sam, a phone call I got a few days ago. Everything points back there."

"What are you talking about? What phone call?"

"Some private detective said I might be interested in a personal matter having to do with Las Vegas."

"Well, what was it?"

"In the end he wouldn't say."

~ ~ ~

Fear is a funny thing. It strikes quickly and can paralyze you for hours—days even—with its complex of self-doubt, anger, and craven abjectness. For perhaps the first time in her life, Helena tasted all this and spent a tortured day and night in its grip. Someone knew something about what happened in Las Vegas. Did they know about her? Could she really tell Brad what she saw, even the doctored version she had shared with Angela? After their conversation the previous day, how could she inflict this new impropriety on him? Would his mother have to know?

When Helena decided to tell him—*had* to tell him, she felt better. It would deflect the suspicion he might be harboring about her and Sam Porter. And she wasn't worried about Sam somehow betraying her. She had a lot of leverage over him right now; he had even more to lose than she did. Sam wanted Angela *and* her, and the money and power that came from his new status. Helena knew something about using that against him if he tried to push her out of the way.

It seemed to her that someone, that private detective most likely, had traced the phone call Angela made back to Sharples Communications. Angela had made that call from the lobby of the Tremont building. Probably as a fishing expedition, this man called Brad about it. But in the end, so what? She and Angela had no real connection to the murders. They only knew what they knew. Helena's dread had been an overreaction. She could make this right for all of them.

Telling Angela what she intended to do was the easy part. By making a clean breast of it to Brad, she would ease her sister's mind about deceiving him on that awful day. In the end, they would all agree that the phone call to Wanda Buckley was the right thing to do, even though it should have been Helena making the call, back there in Las Vegas. If worse came to worse, she'd be brave and speak to the police about it. But she knew Brad would have none of that. The publicity, after all.

The big confession scene played out well. Helena, Brad and Angela sat around the island in the faux country kitchen with the skillets and pots hanging over them on the black cast iron rack.

"I ran, Brad," she said. "I couldn't help it. I was totally unnerved at what I saw. I stumbled out of the yard and just drove away. It was cowardly, and I'm ashamed of myself."

Tears sprung to his eyes. He took Helena's hand and pressed it to his chest.

"Sweetheart, I hope you can put this out of your mind. We never have to discuss it again. I don't think you're a coward, I think you're brave and good. And Angela, I can't thank you enough for helping us out like that."

It was as though Helena had scripted it.

~ ~ ~

The wedding followed her script as well. The strapping young husband kissed the angelic bride among friends and loved ones, surrounded by banks of flowers in pastel hues, with music from a string quartet surging in counterpoint to the ceremony and the wedding vows. After this spectacle, Helena thought that she and Brad might as well get hitched in Las Vegas by an Elvis impersonator in some tacky chapel with his mother as witness, clucking her disapproval.

But she had promised herself not to be bitter, hadn't she? And she knew that the intense level of activity and planning had been good for her. What with the wedding preparations to coordinate and the guest list to monitor and resolve, she hadn't had time to think for a week.

Society Wedding of the Year, the headlines would proclaim. Relatives came from as far away as New England, despite the short notice. A mix of reporters, photographers and rubberneckers filled the street outside, and two television transmission trucks flanked the gates to the drive, but they hadn't invaded the grounds or been overly intrusive. Making use of Brad's influence with the press and the police department, Helena had managed to keep the tide of onlookers at bay without inconveniencing the guests or the service people.

Inside the house, Helena was just allowing herself a breather and a cocktail. The reception line had ended, the guests dispersing to the terrace and library. It wouldn't be long before Angela and Sam would be looking to steal away, she thought. At that point, she could finally kick off her shoes and crash. Since morning, she had been afraid that the tension between her and Sam would become obvious. Every time they spoke, he seemed to be gloating. His manner had become triumphant, and she wanted to slap his evil, grinning face. But it was his day, too, and she couldn't avoid him entirely.

Sam sought her out in the crowd while she was schmoozing guests. She had just finished speaking to Ivan Chitworth, a nice but rather effeminate relative of hers from Newport, Rhode Island.

"Well, sister," he said, "now that we're related, I'm looking forward to being a real brother to you."

As he leaned in for a kiss, she pulled away. He was only trying to be congenial, but she wasn't having any.

"Related? I don't think so. What's the relationship of a brother-in-law to a step-sister? Sounds kind of phony, Sam, doesn't it? Like everything else about you and me."

He set his jaw at that, let his glare burn into her, then smiled and walked over to his grotesque little friend Mickey, the one he asked her to invite to the wedding. Just then the housekeeper came up to tell her a gentleman had come around to the service entrance requesting to speak to Miss Sharples. She didn't care for his looks and wasn't sure what to say.

"All right, Esther. I'll take care of it. Just make sure that the caterer is completely set up in the great room. "

A pudgy fellow with a hangdog manner was standing outside the service entrance, hat in hand, looking hot and out of sorts. He smiled feebly when Helena opened the screen door and introduced herself as Angela's sister. His jowls seemed to rattle as he spoke.

"Sorry to intrude," he said. "I represent an out-of-town client and I need to speak to Miss Angela Sharples. May I ask what the event is? All those reporters . . . "

"It's Mrs. Porter now, not Miss Sharples. This is her wedding day."

Pedro Brunetti's face took on an expression so alarming, Helena wondered if he would take a stroke. But when she made a gesture to help him inside, he backed up and shook his head. Taking a moment to pull himself together, he kept his eyes down and bit his lower lip.

"Ma'am, I'm really sorry to bother you. My business

can wait, of course. A wedding, after all."

"Why don't you leave your card, or a message?"

"Oh, time for that later. Such a pedestrian affair, you understand."

And he was gone, striding away quickly for a fat man. Before an hour was out, Helena had forgotten all about him.

CHAPTER 17

GETTING LUCKY

PEDRO HAD THE IMPRESSION reporters hung out together at certain bars, like cops, but it seems the new breed was different. At least this crew was. For all he knew they drank as much as ever, but in the new, diversified workplace, they seemed to go their own way more. Not a tight bunch, apparently. Well, if it didn't work like you see in the movies, he'd have to earn his pay and think harder about the problem. And if that didn't work, he'd have to get lucky.

It so happened Pedro got lucky when he stopped moping about in the lobby of the Tremont Building and twirled out the revolving door one afternoon. He was determined to forget the whole business for a while, maybe take a nap back in his hotel room. He hit the sidewalk and spotted a lunchroom called the Blue Plate a block away to the left. Stopping for a sandwich, he thought to ask the middle-aged waitress if any workers from Sharples Communications ate there.

"Sure they do," she said. "Reporters come in here all the time."

"What I figured," was all he said by way of reply.

For the next week, Pedro was a fixture at the Blue Plate. He often called himself Pete Brown when he was out and about, which he did here. Before long he knew Eleanor, the regular waitress, and Tyrone, the cook. Every day, he dropped in for coffee break and lunch, friendly and outgoing, chatting with patrons whenever possible.

An occasional topic of conversation for the Sharples crew was a new initiative for product management at the newspaper. Pedro's ears pricked up one lunch period when a reporter he had already met mentioned that a consultant, whose name was Sam, was at loggerheads with some editor. Having already established his persona as a kind of buttinsky, Pedro piped up.

"Sam? Sam who?"

"Guy's name is Sam Porter," the reporter said.

The hairs on Pedro's neck rose up. There *was* a connection between Sharples and his boy from Las Vegas.

It proved easy enough to trace Porter to the Prado Hotel off Market Street. And when Mickey Cullion showed up one day, he had two-thirds of a trifecta in place. Now what about the mystery woman and her phone call? Brad Styles might know something, but Pedro wasn't ready to confront him until he had more to work with.

The prize question, of course, concerned Sam Porter. What was a low-rent casino dealer doing in a responsible management position for a big time San Francisco newspaper? Brad Styles would know him, probably had a say in hiring him. Did he know there was a Las Vegas connection? Pedro thought he must, which would explain why he tried to pump him for information when they spoke earlier.

He was spinning his wheels again, which brought him back to the only other executive's name he knew, Angela Sharples. Did he dare approach the eminent Miss Sharples? He had it in mind to ask her a few discreet questions. He understood she wasn't intimately involved in the day-to-day operation of Sharples Communications, but as president she would have a stake in making sure everything was above board with important functions like product management.

That bright idea fell apart when he went out there

on her damn wedding day and learned her new name was *Porter*. Her sister came to the door and delivered the punch line. She was a dark-haired beauty with a great figure and a condescending manner.

~ ~ ~

Pedro was staggered. Every corner he turned was revealing a new complication, a disturbing facet of the case he felt unprepared to deal with. Nevertheless, he related everything he had learned to Wanda Buckley, letting her know he thought Sam Porter was very likely the boyfriend Lana had told her about.

"Which I can't prove, you understand, but he's a big, good-looking fellow, and he left Las Vegas around the time of the murders."

"I'm coming to San Francisco," she said. "Tomorrow."

"But Wanda, why? What good would it do?"

"Everybody else is there, why not me!"

"I mean what could you possibly do here?"

"I could just *be* there. What can I do *here* except be frustrated waiting for you to call?"

"Yes. Well, if you come, let me know where you're going to stay."

"Get me a room at your hotel, Pedro. Both our fat asses will be on the expense account. We'll make a great team."

"M-m-m. Laurel and Hardy were a great team, Wanda."

"Don't crack wise, Pedro."

The thought of them working together was distasteful to Pedro. After Wanda flew in to San Francisco and got settled at the Junipero Arms, she spent half her day questioning him about the case and complaining about expenses. When she wasn't driving him crazy, she would commandeer a bellboy and have him play hi-lo-jack with her. And she cheated. He thanked God he booked her a room on a different floor. Most days he managed to avoid her.

The most significant thing that happened about then was a conversation he had with Janeway's boss Viejo. This guy was interested in Pedro's investigation of the phone call and his discovery of Sam Porter in San Francisco.

"I know I can't prove anything," he told Viejo, "but I'd sure like to see Porter's personnel records at the Riviera."

"We got a warrant and I had Janeway pull them, Brunetti. It doesn't tell us much, so we're looking into whether he has priors. Listen, we've got a small DNA sample, a blood stain at the scene that doesn't match either victim."

"Never heard about that."

"Right. We held it back from the press. I'm telling you because I'd like your cooperation on something. The chief here won't authorize a trip to San Francisco until Porter is back from his honeymoon. When I do get over there, I'll follow Porter until he drops a cigarette butt or something in a public place. Then we'll have something to compare."

"What do you need from me?" Pedro asked.

"Just give us a holler if Mickey Cullion leaves town. I don't expect you to tail him, but you can keep your eyes open for me."

"Okay, I will. Now do me a favor, Viejo. I know you looked at that phone call to Wanda Buckley on the day of the murders. What do you make of it?"

"Well, the call came in after the estimated time of death. Someone in Vegas who knew Wanda Buckley must have seen something, got scared and asked a lady friend in San Francisco to phone it in."

"Well, sure. But does it connect to Sam Porter?"

"That's wishful thinking, Brunetti. You have to

figure it as coincidence."

"I guess. But it doesn't sit right."

"Wait a minute, wait a minute . . . Who did you say Porter married?"

"Angela Sharples. Big socialite here."

"Uh-huh . . . I'm thinking of something I saw on the passenger manifest for the flight Porter took out of Las Vegas . . . I got it right here . . . Flight was about half full and he was in first class . . . Yeah, here we go. There was a Helena Sharples Swann in tourist class."

"Shit. That's the sister!"

"Bingo!"

"What bingo? I still don't make a connection with the phone call to Wanda."

"What if it was Helena Swann saw something and called ahead to San Francisco. Could explain why Wanda got the phone call from there."

"But if Porter's our boy for the murders, why would his future sister-in-law call somebody to squeal?"

"Nice little problem to work out, hunh?"

"Yeah. And while I'm at it I might as well figure out why he was in first class and she was in tourist."

"Being careful, maybe?"

"To me it sounds more like they didn't know each other then. Which means you got a witness and a murderer who just happened to meet each other and . . ."

"Must be fate, Brunetti. She introduces him to her sister who marries him. Shit, for all the sense that makes, maybe we'd both better start over."

Viejo was laughing at him, but as it happened, he was on the money. Fate had provided the case with its defining moment. And they had been lucky to make the connection. Not that either of them had it figured out yet.

CHAPTER 18

COMPLICATIONS

MICKEY CULLION SAW BRUNETTI in town one afternoon when he went to meet Sam at the Prado. Cautious, he never went directly inside the hotel without checking first. There was a second-hand bookstore across the street at the corner where he could watch the hotel entrance for a while from the storefront window. Sam was the bold guy who took the big view and the direct action. Mickey was the cautious one, the little sneak thief always on the lookout for complications.

The fat P.I. from Las Vegas was his first complication. Pedro walked down the street past the Prado and crossed to the other side after glancing into the lobby window. Mickey figured he'd be taking a position nearby in some doorway or other. Thinking it over, he came to the sorry conclusion that Pedro Brunetti must already know both of them were in town.

Mickey slipped out of the bookstore and went the other way. Sam wasn't too worried when he called him from a pay phone a few minutes later. He was just two days away from his wedding and had the world all wrapped up in a pretty package.

"He may have already seen both of us, Mickey, but so what? We both have legitimate jobs and he has nothing on me from Las Vegas."

"Okay, but who's he working for and why?"

"I know who. Wanda Buckley. Lana was a good friend of hers. The old bitch is trying to track me down. Count on it."

"I thought you said the old lady don't know you."

"I never met her, but Lana was always talking about her. She might know my name."

"What if a cop shows up asking you questions?"

"I dated her a couple of times. End of story. Real sorry to hear about the murder."

"Don't say it like that. This is freakin' me out."

"Relax, Mickey. I've got this covered."

"What does that mean?"

"First sign of real trouble we'll be gone. And I'll have the money to bankroll us."

It seems Sam had authorization to hire vendors and have checks issued at work. Given two weeks, he figured they could leave San Francisco with forty grand. That was news to Mickey, and larceny on that scale scared him. On the other hand, they both knew good places to lay low. Sam could easily enough fake a trail to Montana that would seem plausible to the cops while he went south instead, and Mickey could get off to Baja. After a time, they would meet up someplace. But how far could Mickey trust him? He told Sam the money would have to be divided *before* they split up.

"Mickey, all this is just a contingency plan. I don't want to run unless we have to. For now, tail Brunetti for me, find out where he stays, who he sees."

In addition, Sam wanted him to go to work as usual while he was on his honeymoon. Mickey could ask the new product agents for gofer work and keep his ears open for scuttlebutt.

On his wedding day, Sam threw in another task, telling him to keep tabs on Helena's visits to Brad at the office. Mickey figured he was banging the sister as well as the bride, but he couldn't for the life of him see why he liked that snotty Helena. At the wedding, she reacted to him the way you'd react to a cockroach in the shower. The complications were piling up, and Mickey's stomach was in knots.

CHAPTER 19

JUST ANOTHER WEAPON

THE RECEPTION WAS OVER, the guests gone, the street outside the mansion finally cleared of spectators and press. The newlyweds had a tight schedule to make, so their good-byes were rushed. Helena had called ahead to have the condo in Kauai ready for them on their wedding night. It hadn't been opened since before Sam Sharples died. Before leaving, Angela embraced Helena with great warmth, taking time to praise her efforts.

"It was perfect, Helena," she said. "I can't thank you enough."

"Who could deserve it more?" she lied.

Helena had to allow Sam a kiss this time while Angela said goodbye to Brad.

"Just right here on the cheek, Sam."

"Of course, sister."

"Will I ever get used to you as a brother?"

"I'm counting on it."

"First, Sam as a father," she sighed, "and now Sam as a brother."

"With one difference," he said. "His first name was Samuel, mine is Samson."

"Samson Porter?"

"That's right."

"Well, Samson, it's time for you to shuffle off with Delilah."

He smiled, but shook his head with emphasis.

"Unh-uh, Angela won't ever be my Delilah."

Helena didn't bother asking who would be. She was too worried about being alone with Brad now that everyone was gone. His suspicions were mounting again, and she knew today's burdens weren't over yet. After surveying the downstairs rooms and giving instructions to the cleaning crew, she asked Esther to serve coffee in the library. Brad seemed preoccupied, so she spoke first when they had settled in.

"It's good to see Angela so happy," she said. "But thank God it's over. I'm totally worn out."

"M-m-m. You must be. I was beginning to think I'd never see you alone again."

There it was again, she thought, that note of dissatisfaction.

"I'm sorry, Brad. I know there's a lot bothering you. Can we talk about it? I haven't meant to neglect you."

His eyes searched her face, probing. Not hostile, but unsure. Was he doubting her? Passing a hand over his face, he tried to smile and failed.

"Yes, there is a lot happening just now," he said. "There are problems at work I haven't been able to talk to Angela about, for obvious reasons. But what's wrong with us, Helena, is the distance you've put between us. We haven't even made love for weeks."

She wanted to object, but Brad's eyes were fixed on hers. Humiliated, she looked away.

He was right. Since Sam had come to town, they hadn't made love. Her first impulse was to make up for it right away, but that wouldn't help. Not then at least.

"Brad, I didn't realize . . . I'm sorry."

"So am I. The worst of it is the feeling that you're a different woman now. Do you realize how changed you are since you came back from Las Vegas?"

"But Brad . . . the divorce . . . Angela and the wedding—you've got to make some allowances."

"I assure you I have, Helena. We've always known about your ambition to have a big, exciting life, you've talked about it since you were a kid. Well, you're just as restless now as you ever were. I know you love me, but what kind of love is it really? You're not content with me. You've other plans, I think."

Every word was true. But she wasn't ready to give Brad up. Beyond the security and stability he represented for her, he was goodness itself, and maybe the last chance for her to embrace goodness and decency as a way of life. Sam had upset this applecart, and Helena had nothing at all to show for it, except the power to expose his charade and reveal him to Angela. Whichever way she turned, danger loomed. If she turned to Brad, she should be honest with him, but she couldn't predict the consequences. If she kept playing the double game, Sam would surely bring her down.

She wept. The tears came easily, and yet she couldn't say whether it was real emotion or just another weapon she had picked up along the way.

"Brad, please give me a chance to prove you wrong. Can't you get away from work for a few days so we can spend time together? That's what we need now."

"You may be right, Helena, but I'm too tired to think about it. We'll talk real soon. I'm going now."

She hadn't even time to dry her tears before he was out the door.

CHAPTER 20

A DISTURBING PATTERN

THE PROJECT WASN'T GOING half badly. Brad Styles was looking at the budget runs, and they were in decent shape. Overall progress was more than satisfactory. Sam's abilities were confirmed now, but there were concerns about his people skills, his ethics, and his background. The way he dazzled Brad at first caused him to let his guard down. Here was someone with a positive attitude who wanted a chance at helping him boost circulation for the newspaper. He had been looking at the sad, declining statistics for a long time, and everyone concerned was predicting more losses for each succeeding year.

So he had overlooked the gaps in Sam's resume in favor of his potential. The reference check, when Human Resources got around to it, was another matter. Some things were fine, some things looked like dead ends. Two problems stood out. The college he graduated from was a junior college that awarded only two-year associate degrees. Well, he wouldn't be the first to fib about that. Worse perhaps, the college was no longer accredited.

It was that job as member of a product team that worried Brad most. Blue Cross of Arizona verified his employment, but let it slip that it was part of an experimental program funded by the state. They didn't supply any more information, and H.R. suspected that the positions were more like subsidized internships than serious jobs. Not very good for his primary reference.

His team at Sharples respected him, but a couple of

editors were wary of his methods. A senior female editor wouldn't meet with him further on the basis of feeling "uncomfortable." She wasn't filing a complaint, but she didn't like being in his presence and would only work with him through others. This was a disturbing pattern after such a short time on the job, and Brad called him on it.

"I'm sorry about this," Sam told him. "I can be too insistent, I know that's a fault. Give me a chance to adjust my manner, the way I interact with people. You know, I'd like to accept the complaints at face value and move on rather than debate them. And I'll be more than happy to make a personal apology to anyone I've offended."

This was an excellent approach, and he caught Brad off guard again by having exactly the right attitude. But things Brad couldn't pin down bothered him as much, if not more. The phone call he received after hiring Sam turned out to be from a private investigator in Las Vegas. He left messages with the man's answering service that were never returned. Had this something to do with Sam Porter? And did the tension he sensed in Helena have something to do with him? She had, after all, shared that flight with him from Las Vegas. Besides, she had introduced him into his life and Angela's.

Somehow it all started in Las Vegas. What was it? What happened there besides that awful scene Helena saw?

The day after the wedding, Brad asked her to have lunch with him in town. They had been through that emotional scene after the wedding reception, but he still wasn't in the mood to patch things up. Rather, he thought it best to face their problems squarely. Helena claimed to love him, though he doubted her. He always knew his passion for her was greater than hers for him, but in the past it didn't matter somehow. Now, watching Angela's complete devotion to Sam, a man he thought not good enough for her, made him want more from Helena. Would she be ready for that?

CHAPTER 21

WHAT BRAD DESERVES

HELENA WAS DETERMINED not to lose Brad. When he called, she was chastened and demure. She wouldn't be able to tell you how much of this was an act, because she had long ago lost the ability to simply be herself in some unthinking fashion. In her mind, life had cast her in a role that called for a skilled actress. That's who she was. It didn't diminish her that she used her passions and her intelligence as she did, emphasizing them now, denying or denigrating them at other times. It was all in service to her need to manipulate those around her and negotiate the best possible deal for herself. Helena Swann was the sum of all this and perhaps more.

Sam was the first man to test her ability to act her way through a relationship. And now some change in her demeanor or attitude had conveyed itself to Brad, who didn't like what he saw. But it wasn't too late for them. Not yet.

Brad was a man who was wary of change. His life revolved around duty and responsibility. These were the things Helena loved him for, and these would be the things she would have to embrace. The roles she would need to fulfill for him were those of wife, gracious hostess, trusted advisor and, eventually, mother to his children. Brad's own mother was the exemplar in his life for those virtues, and he deserved no less from Helena. Despite her rebellious ways, he saw these qualities in her at one time. She had to revive his faith.

During lunch, they talked about the wedding and her houseguest, Ivan Chitworth, who had stayed over.

She told him Ivan had taken an early flight to Boston and would meet with a friend there before driving to Newport, where he lived at Dismas Cottage, his mother's estate.

"Ivan's what . . . your cousin?" Brad asked.

"I always called him that. Angela's and Ivan's mothers were sisters. Old Newporters. I haven't visited there in years. We stayed at Dismas Cottage any number of summers when we were little."

"Ivan seemed . . . well, gay."

"Oh, yes. I adored him as a little girl. An *unrequited* love."

They laughed. Brad had loosened up, and Helena felt much better. When he became serious, it was to talk first about problems at Sharples Communications. Naturally, Sam was at the root of these.

The good and bad of Sam were evident to Brad now. Disgruntled staff members, ethical lapses and a problematic background were set off against good progress and unquestionable energy. It occurred to Helena that she could guide Brad here, be that trusted advisor he needed.

"Darling," she said, putting her hand on his, "don't shoulder this alone. We've all seen that Sam is a kind of force of nature. Controlling him can't be your responsibility alone. You should back off as far as you can for now and speak to Angela when she gets back. She has to be your ally in this for Sam's good and the good of the company. And if you want me to broach it to her first, well why not? I'm her sister after all, and I care deeply about both of you."

His eyes registered surprise as she spoke. Having finished his lunch, he wiped his mouth and set his napkin aside.

"Helena, I don't think I've ever heard your opinion on my work before. Thanks for the advice. I think you're right. In fact, I'm sure you are."

It was a good start. By letting him initiate the conversation, she was able to concentrate on him and his needs. She hoped he'd get around to their personal life, so she could follow his lead there as well, but a city supervisor came over during coffee and wanted to talk about a municipal function Brad would be attending next month. This cut into their time together. He had to get back to the office right after lunch.

Still, she had become hopeful. As they parted, Brad promised to drop over that evening. Helena was determined to be ready for him.

CHAPTER 22

BURY THE HATCHET

THE SATURDAY MORNING after Sam left with his bride for Hawaii, Mickey Cullion was keeping watch near Pedro Brunetti's hotel and nearly fell asleep from the lack of action there. Finally, around ten o'clock, Pedro came strolling out with an old lady in tow. She wasn't as big as him, but pretty close, with a red, round face and gray-brown hair all piled up and around in what Mickey wanted to say was a French twist. And talking, talking, talking.

If he didn't know better, he might have thought they were married. Pedro was nodding his head and looking like a rat does when the cat's nearby and he doesn't see a hole to run for. Mickey had never met Wanda Buckley, but he recognized the old bag from all the news coverage after the Las Vegas murders.

They wound up at Wendy's for breakfast. Damn, he thought, who goes to freakin' Wendy's for breakfast?

Afterwards, Pedro took off, and Wanda went back to the hotel alone. Although Mickey was supposed to be tailing Brunetti, he was sure Sam would want to know what Wanda Buckley was up to in San Francisco. Which is exactly what he said when he called Mickey from the honeymoon condo on Kauai.

"Find out her schedule, when she goes out, what time she gets back. Find a pattern I can use. I'll have to talk to her someday when the P.I. isn't around."

"You gotta be kidding. What good will that do?"

"I can be very convincing. I'll tell her I know the guy she's after is in L.A. It'll be enough of a diversion to screw Brunetti up. It'll give me more time."

"It might work, but what if Brunetti asks her for a

detailed description of the guy she talked to. He'll figure it's you."

"Yeah, you've got a point. Let me think about that. Anyway, I'm not worried about this piss-ant investigation of theirs. If they had something, they'd bring the cops in. That's when it gets serious."

Mickey wasn't so sure, but he didn't have a better plan. The other thing he told Sam about was Helena stopping in to see Brad the day after the wedding. It must've been just a lunch date, because he saw Brad later at the office.

"Have you staked out the house at all?" he asked.

"Man, you're asking a lot. People in high rent districts aren't used to dudes hanging around outside in old, beat-up cars. They tend to call the police about that stuff."

"All right, Mickey. Forget about it. See you when I get back."

~ ~ ~

Mickey had expected Sam's call from Hawaii. Helena Swann getting in touch was a horse of a different flavor. His eyes bugged out when he was called to the phone at work, and it was Helena asking to meet him for a drink. Leery as he was about it, saying "no thanks" didn't seem like an option.

She named a high-end hotel bar and suggested five-thirty as a convenient time.

"Okay, Mrs. Swann, but maybe you should tell me what this is about."

"Yes," she said, "I suppose you've every right to be suspicious. I was very abrupt with you at the wedding and I'd like to apologize for that. I realize you're Sam's friend and he's part of our family now. So I felt we could bury the hatchet over a drink and some conversation."

Jesus, he thought, does anybody really talk like that? And what could she want? Helena Swann certainly wasn't going to recruit him into her social set, so she must be planning to pump him for information. What the hell, he thought, why not go along with it? If she had a game to play, he might as well find out what it was.

He showed up at five o'clock, a half hour early. First, he looked the hotel over to see where the entrance to the bar was and to figure what direction she'd be coming from. Then he planned where to sit so her back would be to the entrance while he would face it. Finally, he checked out the lobby before returning to the bar.

A waiter approached him, and Mickey ordered a drink. He let the fellow know he was waiting for someone. It wasn't long before Helena appeared at the bar entrance, stopping a moment before waltzing in with a kind of sweeping motion—all legs and arms and head held high—the way he always imagined a society broad would do it.

Out of the corner of his eye, he could see the waiter and bartender do a double take—thinking what in hell is *she* doing with the little dude.

"Hello, Mrs. Swann," he said. "Would you like to order a drink?"

"Why yes, I'd like that," she said

Mickey raised his arm and snapped his fingers for the waiter, just because he had always wanted to play a scene like this.

"The lady will have a drink, waiter," he said. "What will it be, Mrs. Swann?"

"Vodka martini with a lemon twist, please."

Mickey wanted to bust out laughing after getting his line off. In his mind, he was some punk in a movie romancing a pretty lady. But she didn't have any interest in sharing the fantasy.

"I'll try not to keep you very long, Mickey. You know I'm sorry for treating you badly the other day. I was trying to make everything perfect for Angela and I guess I became rather tense and fretful."

"No offense, Mrs. Swann. I understand."

"Please call me Helena," she said, not meaning it in the least.

He nodded without replying. The waiter served her drink, and she raised her glass for a sip. For the first time, she looked him directly in the eye.

"You've met Brad Styles, my fiancé?"

"I know who he is. I've seen him at work."

"We had a discussion recently about a number of problems at work. I thought you might be able to help us. I'm sure you know I don't work at Sharples, but Brad does and my sister is the president. The situation is rather delicate because the problems involve Sam Porter. Since Sam is your friend, I thought you might want to help him."

"Sam may be my friend . . . Helena . . . but he's also my boss. What could I do for him that his wife or sister-in-law couldn't?"

Mickey figured she was surprised that he was stepping up to the plate and hitting them to the outfield. But she was no slouch either.

"I often find that an old friend knows how to give advice better than a relative, Mickey. Sam is pretty headstrong."

"Guess you're right about that. Well, what kind of advice would you like me to give Sam?"

"Has he called you from Hawaii?"

"If you don't mind, I'd sure appreciate it if you'd answer my question first."

He noticed Helena's jaw tighten at that, but she hid it well with a shrug and a smile.

"Sam is getting good results, but he's alienating the people he has to work with. Brad has talked to him about it, of course. You've probably heard about the problems, Mickey. Just encourage him along those lines—you know, playing nice. I'm sure you're a good friend and he'll listen to you. He's got a bright future if he'll cooperate with Brad."

Mickey made a kind of futile gesture with one hand and shook his head.

"I make nine bucks an hour, Mrs. Swann. Your sister runs a big organization with your fiancé and they employ personnel specialists, consultants like Sam, all kinds of big shots. You gotta pardon me, but I don't get it. There's no way it makes sense that I'm the guy who can make Sam change his ways."

Both of her well-tended eyebrows shot up.

"Your friend may be the president's husband, but his job references didn't check out very well and I suspect yours may not either. Considering the situation on both sides, neither Brad nor I want to make any difficulties for you. We just want the problems I've told you about to disappear. Sam can do that if he has a mind to, and you can help."

"So why isn't Mr. Brad here? Why did he ask you to carry the load?"

"I'm not sure that is any of your business, but I asked him to let me handle it unofficially. If he took direct action with you, there would have to be a record of it at work."

Now Mickey had to play along or walk away. He had the feeling if he stalled her with one more question, she'd walk.

"It's my turn to apologize, Mrs. Swann. I don't mean to put you off, but this isn't really up my alley. Is it your idea I should try to influence Sam but keep this conversation confidential?"

"Why, no. I can see what you mean, though. No, I'm not trying to be underhanded, I would expect you to tell Sam we met and talked. I'm really trying to save him some grief. Angela called me from Hawaii, but Sam didn't get on the line. If he had, I might have said something along these lines. Did he call you?"

"Yes, and I'm sorry I wouldn't answer that before."

"Well, maybe we can stop fencing now and relax."

Not fuckin' likely, Mickey thought. They tried to make small talk, but he was nervous by then, and he was no good at it anyway. Although she posed a lot of questions about his past and Sam's, he felt sure he knew what information Sam had fed her, which made that part easy. Helena left about six o'clock, but not before Mickey saw Pedro Brunetti's fat ass walking by the bar entrance. Christ, he thought, somebody should have taught him how to tail better than that.

Was Brunetti just following him around for Wanda Buckley, or were Helena Swann and Brad Styles cooperating with his investigation? Oh man, what was Sam gonna say about this?

CHAPTER 23

SOMETHING ABOUT LAS VEGAS

AFTER HER LUNCH with Brad, Helena came home and changed into loungewear. With Angela in Hawaii, Esther had taken the week off, leaving her alone in the house. The day had been typical San Francisco weather, the fog lasting until late morning when the sun peeked through to brighten the landscape. The evening promised to be warm and pleasant. Helena preferred to throw open the windows and leave the air conditioning off whenever possible, which she did. She had several hours to think and plan their evening together—Brad's and hers.

It needed to be intimate, personal, and ultimately romantic. Yet she didn't want it to seem too thought out. Brad would have to make the advances. If he was holding back, her task would be to lower his defenses without seeming to play the seductress. He mustn't suspect she was trying to win him back, she thought. Rather, he must reach the conclusion that he wanted her as much as ever because he could place his trust in her. Her love must seem real to him again.

Brad pulled up to the house right on time, as always. After they settled themselves on the terrace with tall glasses of iced tea, he took her hand and thanked her again for her advice at lunch.

"You know, I think I've been unfair to you, darling."

"Brad, you don't have to explain, not after the way I've neglected you."

"Still, there are things I need to get off my mind. Something happened in Las Vegas, Helena. The private detective who called me—Brunetti—wanted to talk about it, then he backed off. I called his answering service more than once, but he doesn't return my calls. Until now, I've had the uneasy feeling that whatever it was involved Sam Porter and possibly you."

"I don't know about Sam, but what about those awful murders? Could someone have seen me at Wanda Buckley's house?"

"I thought of that, but why would a private investigator be involved? That would be a police matter. And even if he is interested, if he's playing some game, why not call you directly?"

"You're right, of course. If it were a case of blackmail, the pretext is rather thin. And he would have made a demand by now."

"Exactly. And if it's about Sam, why not tell *me* what was on his mind?"

"If he wasn't going to tell you what happened, why call you at all?"

"Well, he may have called just to see what kind of reaction he got. If that was it, it must have been obvious to him that he pushed a button. As soon as I heard *Las Vegas*, I was alarmed."

"Brad, you have so much to do at work, let me call this Brunetti. Let's see if he'll talk to me."

"Oh, don't get involved in this, sweetheart."

"Nonsense, you just give me that phone number. I have nothing in the world to hide and neither do you. If this is about Sam for some reason, you should know it sooner rather than later. Like you, I'll probably find out nothing. But what's the harm in trying?"

Very likely, Brad thought he was indulging her by acquiescing. He said she should call his assistant for the telephone number.

The rest of the night was strictly personal. They relaxed, called out for pizza, watched television and got back to the kind of quiet intimacy they had before Las Vegas and Sam Porter and the inquisitive private eye spoiled it. As much as she would have liked to, Helena couldn't claim that their lovemaking was explosive or even satisfying. In truth, it was the same as always. It made Brad very happy and content. It left her wanting more. Nevertheless, she was delighted to have him back.

~ ~ ~

Before picking up the phone, Helena focused her thoughts on this Brunetti person, trying to devine his motives. A private detective calls the executive director of a large corporation and wants to talk about something 'personal' that occurred in Las Vegas. Well, both Sam Porter and she had connections to Sharples Communications. Furthermore, they both had a connection to Brad. She decided if this was about her, she'd be able to handle it. If it was about Sam . . . well, she wanted to be the first to know.

When the answering service told her Mr. Brunetti was out of town, she asked if he retrieved his calls on a regular basis.

"Oh yes," the voice said. "He calls in almost every day. I'll be sure to tell him you called, Mrs. Swann."

"Please let him know that I wish to do business with him," she said.

Her remark was meant to be ambiguous. Whether his intent was blackmail or a simple request for information, she wanted to convey her desire to treat with him.

Brunetti called back within a few hours. It was late morning and she was in her bedroom, having just stepped out of the shower, naked except for the black and white patterned towel tied at her waist.

After pushing the damp hair away from her face, she reached out for the extension on the vanity and picked up.

"Hello?"

"Mrs. Swann, this is Pedro Brunetti. How are you this morning?"

"Very well, thank you."

"Do you remember me, Mrs. Swann?"

"Mr. Brunetti, I only just heard of you two days ago. Brad Styles is my fiancé. He's been trying to get in touch with you."

"I know that, Mrs. Swann. Perhaps you recall the fat man at the service entrance on your sister's wedding day."

"Why yes, yes I do. Well . . . you certainly are a strange detective, Mr. Brunetti. First you call Brad and mystify him. Then you come to my door, ask for my sister and walk away before I can assist you. I hope you intend to explain all this."

"A matter of prudence, Mrs. Swann. My investigation concerns neither you nor your fiancé, nor your sister. Yet every time I followed a lead to Sam Porter, I came up with disturbing new connections."

"What on earth are you talking about?"

"Mrs. Swann, Saint Paul said *God hath chosen the foolish things of the world to confound the wise.* A rather crazy coincidence led me to find out that Sam Porter was in San Francisco. I don't want to get into that, but I will tell you I'm investigating Mr. Porter on a serious matter that happened in Las Vegas."

"That would concern my sister, of course. Who is your client? If this is so serious, why aren't the police involved?"

"I seem to have information that the police lack at this time. I can't reveal my client's name, of course."

"Well Mr. Brunetti, this is all very confusing. If you have something you wish to convey to either my sister or her husband, please tell me now."

"You'll recall, I'm sure, that your message said you wished to do business with me. That was an interesting choice of words, Mrs. Swann. Did you have something particular in mind?"

There it was. Pedro Brunetti was not beyond a little business proposition from a third party. Helena wasn't about to discuss money on the telephone, so they arranged to meet on the Marina Park waterfront late that afternoon. She was certain his investigation was along the lines of casino fraud. Mickey had told her something just the previous day when she asked about his job in Las Vegas. Both he *and* Sam worked in Las Vegas, something Sam had never mentioned. He told us he was at leisure in Las Vegas, having gotten a bequest from an uncle's estate. In reality, he was a dealer at the Riviera. A dealer under suspicion by the gaming commission, perhaps? That would explain the 'bequest' and the sudden compulsion to leave town.

Her goal now was to find out if Brunetti would end his investigation of Sam Porter in consideration of a . . . monetary settlement. She thought this would help Angela, Brad and Sharples Communications. And Sam Porter, of course. Which one of those good deeds was uppermost in her mind was a fleeting thought that she managed to push away.

CHAPTER 24

SUFFICIENT CONSIDERATION

AFTER HIS TALK WITH LIEUTENANT VIEJO, Pedro Brunetti had gone through Wanda Buckley's real estate transactions and rental records. Starting with paperwork from around the time of the murders, it wasn't long before he knew that Helena Swann had rented a condo suite from her. With that connection established, it seemed highly likely that Mrs. Swann had something to do with that phone call from San Francisco. He didn't mention this to Wanda, not being able to prove anything, but it was on his mind when he prepared to meet with Helena.

He hoped to find out a few things before they made any deal. Did she suspect Porter was a murderer and wish to protect him anyway? Did she have any idea he suspected her of initiating that phone call, and was that part of her idea to do business? At some point he needed her to state her intentions. He was damned if he was going to set a price without knowing what the bribe was for. And just how careful should he be, he wondered. Should he wear a wire?

They met, as agreed, on the beachfront at Marina Park. Once there, he found out what a sharp customer Helena could be. She had a kind of carryall bag with her. And they had barely said hello when she whipped out an extra large pair of men's swim trunks and pointed to a nearby construction site where there was a Porta-Potty.

"You can change right over there, Mr. Brunetti," she said.

Pedro was indignant. "Mrs. Swann, I am not

recording our conversation! Besides, where would I put my clothes?"

"You could easily make a bundle using your suit jacket, Mr. Brunetti."

Nearly speechless, he nevertheless declined. As a distinctly embarrassing compromise, he stripped to the waist and rolled up the pant legs of his trousers before they continued their walk. The sight of his pale, rotund flesh was a chastisement to him. He couldn't ask her to reciprocate as she was already wearing shorts and a minuscule tank top. No possibility of a wire there.

After a beginning like that, there was no need to observe conversational niceties. Pedro asked her to state her business as clearly as possible. Although she tried to turn that around, he cut her short.

"No, ma'am, you'll have to make your proposal or I'll get dressed and leave."

"Oh, *do* get dressed Mr. Brunetti. I'm sure you feel foolish and I'm confident now that you're not wired."

Yes, she's very good at keeping people off balance, he thought. But he also knew that form never trumps substance. And he was the one who had the goods. So he smiled, covered up and rolled his trousers down.

"Now then, Mrs. Swann, you were saying . . . ?"

"You're investigating Sam Porter, and I want you to stop. I'm prepared to offer you five thousand dollars."

"If you think that's sufficient consideration for suppressing knowledge of a felony, I'm afraid I wouldn't agree."

"That's all I can afford."

"Don't try my patience Mrs. Swann. Your sister is a multi-millionaire and so is your fiancé. My client asked for certain proofs, which I've obtained. What is done with my research is none of my business, but I'm sure the police will be interested. Thirty thousand dollars would inspire me to give you the research and abandon the case."

"First give me an outline of the allegations."

"Don't you know? How very odd!"

"Oh, I'm nearly sure casino fraud is involved, but I want more specifics."

Pedro was able to mask his surprise. Just as well for me, he thought, that she doesn't suspect the worst.

"Well . . . I'm sorry, but the specifics will be in the report. I can't promise there won't be other investigators on his trail, you know. But my report should give you and your family some valuable time to make decisions and react."

"Time for Mr. Porter to disappear, perhaps."

"That would certainly be one option."

"How can I be sure I won't hear from you again?"

"Once our deal is done, I'm in violation of my license. It would be risky to follow up. Besides, all you'll get is a verbal report. I'll read the entire thing to you when you give me the money. Afterwards, I know nothing. My records will be adjusted to omit any real proof. It will take a while before somebody else can dig up that same information."

"Why don't I just tell Mr. Porter to disappear right now?" Clever girl, he thought. But he could bluff as well.

"Hawaii is a small place. If he makes a strange move and doesn't come back when he's supposed to, I'll know about it. That's when my client will receive my full report. As you can see, Mrs. Swann, you haven't much time to raise that money, have you?"

How grand silence can be, he said to himself. Helena Swann looked off into the distance for a moment, turned and began to walk away.

"I'll call you," she said, over her shoulder.

I'm sure you will, he thought! Pedro felt well protected from any repercussions. His dealings with Lieutenant Viejo and Mrs. Buckley had been above board until that moment. Helena Swann was in no danger from him, and any attempt to turn him in wouldn't advance her cause in the least. Or that of her brother-in-law. If she didn't raise the money, she already knew he would proceed. The scenario that blew his mind was her listening to his report after coming across with the thirty thousand. Lord, what in hell does a gal do when she finds out her lover is a psycho killer?

CHAPTER 25

JUMBLED THOUGHTS

HERE SHE WAS AGAIN with that preposterous dilemma. Helena had only just reconciled herself to the good and righteous life with Brad when her thoughts and desires had turned to Sam and his needs. Could she go to Brad for the money? Maybe. After all, he agreed to let her get in touch with Brunetti. Would it make more sense to call Angela in Hawaii? She could authorize a draft on her bank, and Helena would have a report from Brunetti in time for her and Sam to react. Or maybe she should wait and speak to Sam when they came home.

It should have occurred to her right away to let everything follow its natural course. What was this impulse to get involved? Sam Porter was poison for her. Her only logical motive to intervene was to shield Angela. But did logic have anything to do with it?

Helena's thoughts grew more and more jumbled as she tried to think it through. In two short days, she had met with Mickey Cullion for support in getting Sam to change his ways, and had tried to bribe Brunetti for him. In both cases, she started out trying to assist Brad, but ended by scheming how she might either control or help Sam Porter.

She was bone-weary and half-crazy when Angela called to tell her they were coming home early from Hawaii.

"Why, Angela?" she asked.

"A little too quiet in Kauai for Sam, I suspect. He's fretting about the project at work. I tell him to call in and check with Brad, but it's a hands-on thing, I guess. There's only so much tennis and golf you can play when you have Sam's drive."

"And you?"

"Oh, me—I could stay here forever with Sam. But if he can't relax now . . . Hawaii will still be here when the project is over."

"Sure, I understand. Brad and I will be happy to pick you up at the airport, dear. What time will you be arriving?"

Helena couldn't bring herself to speak to Angela about the money she would need to raise to keep her husband out of jail. And she was positive now that she wouldn't bother Brad about it either. Telling Sam he had a problem that he needed to straighten out with Brunetti was her best bet. She would approach him when they got home. After that, she just had to wash her hands of him.

CHAPTER 26

TRUST ISSUES

BY NOW MICKEY CULLION had a complete rundown of Wanda Buckley's routine. She went out to breakfast with or without fat boy around ten, ten-thirty. Back in her room, she made a ton of phone calls most days. At around two o'clock she had a snack, usually from room service. Some days, they'd bring her a bottle of Canadian Club. She ate supper around five-thirty, no later than six, most often in the hotel restaurant. After that she was in for the night, watching television. Brunetti left the hotel in the morning and avoided her as much as he could. Mickey got to know a bellhop who didn't mind feeding him information. This kid played cards with Wanda whenever things were slow. She played for low stakes, and she cheated.

When Sam came home early from the honeymoon, he called Mickey at work and they went over all this. Also, he screwed up his courage to tell Sam about his date with Helena. That led to a long pause, and Mickey began to sweat. Sam claimed to be okay with it, but his tone said otherwise.

"Brad Styles did have a talk with me about that stuff, like she said. Did you believe her that she wants to help?"

"I don't have a lot of experience with high class broads like her. She may have been trying to help, but she was sure as hell trying to pump me for information besides."

"What kind of information?"

"Anything to do with you or me. I don't trust her; she asks too many questions."

"You never trust anybody, Mickey."

"Yeah, well . . . there's one more thing. Don't get mad, just think about it. Brunetti was tailing one of us. I saw him go by when we were in the bar."

"Might not mean anything, but why would he be interested in her—unless they've been in touch? And if they have, why would he need to tail her?"

"Same thing bothers me."

"Tell you what, I'll think about Helena's game, but we're going to fix Brunetti tomorrow night. If he hasn't got a client, he has to drop the case. I'm going to see Wanda Buckley and tell her a story about a guy who went from Vegas to L.A. after the murders."

"Jesus, Sam, we talked about this. Brunetti will know it's you."

"No he won't. I'll have a good disguise. You know—old clothes, mustache, baseball cap. I guarantee he won't know. All you have to do is stay outside the hotel and watch. If he's not out when I go in, you'll go inside to watch his room. Either way, we'll both have cell phones, and you'll call me if I need to get out."

"What'll you do if I have to call you?"

"I'll excuse myself, tell Wanda I'll call later, and go down the service stairs."

"Then what?"

"I'll call her later and finish the story. When I do, he'll have to chase the ghost and we'll be gone within a week. If I'm not rushed, I can get forty thousand."

"One thing Sam, before we even start. I get my half up front. That means *before* we split up."

"Sure, Mickey. There you go with those trust issues again," he laughed.

Trust issues. Yeah, he got that right, Mickey thought. He could already see what might happen. The bastard would embezzle forty grand, claim he could only get twenty, then give Mickey ten.

CHAPTER 27

DREAM GOING DOWN

LIEUTENANT VIEJO

IN HIS JOURNAL, SHOO-FLY doesn't say a whole lot about his honeymoon in Hawaii. He was impressed with the freestanding condo on Kauai with the huge atrium entrance and the five bedrooms clustered around the second floor walkway overlooking the granite foyer. His bride was pretty and responsive, but too passive for his taste. He had to hold back when he made love to her, afraid that she'd whimper and cringe if he let go and plowed her the way he'd like to.

The scenery, the raw-looking red soil, the beaches without number, and the mountain rainforests left him wondering where the city life was. Honolulu and Waikiki would have been more his style. He got into all the daytime physical activity—swimming, snorkeling, tennis, and golf—but every evening was a repeat of the one before. There was dinner with the wife, conversations that went nowhere, sex in the missionary position, and the sense that people back home were looking over his shoulder.

That's what brought him back so quickly. Angela was okay with it, at least she didn't ask too many questions when he told her he was anxious to shepherd that project along at Sharples. What really concerned him, of course, were the law and that fat fuck Brunetti.

An ocean of anger and frustration were building inside him. This was supposed to be his big chance. He was damn good at that job. And Brad had been a halfway decent boss until just before the honeymoon.

He had been agile enough to placate the man about his people skills, but Human Resources had called every damn reference he gave, and now questions were being asked that would be difficult to finesse. Well, if the dream was going down, he figured to get out with a cushion that would enable him to start over somewhere else. Damn, he thought, this was so perfect, so right. Somebody would pay for spoiling it.

Angela and he didn't have two minutes alone that first day back. Brad and Helena met them at the airport and drove them to the Marina district mansion. The girls chatted continuously, as you might expect sisters would after a separation, but Brad was taciturn, cool even. Shoo-fly hadn't expected much more and didn't try to draw him out. When he got a moment alone, he called Mickey and made plans to visit Wanda Buckley in person. That would be kind of fun, he thought, meeting the old broad after hearing so much about her from Lana. But that disguise business he threw out to Mickey, forget that. He'd go in just as he was.

Shortly after noon, Angela went off for a nap after a light lunch on the terrace.

"It must be jet lag," she said. "I just can't keep my eyes open."

Before trotting off upstairs, she came around to everyone for a kiss, lingering a long moment with Shoo-fly, and looking deep into his eyes. It was obvious she wanted him to come with her, but he just smiled.

Not long after, Brad began making a fuss with Helena about visiting his mother, but she put him off with an excuse about helping Angela her first day back.

"I want to go over the household bills and correspondence with her, Brad. Besides, she needs me to help her unpack."

Shoo-fly got the feeling what Helena really wanted was to see him alone. He was right, of course. Brad took off then, kind of huffy and red-faced. Shoo-fly looked on with a big grin, lounging on a terrace chair, legs spread wide.

"Don't gloat, Sam," Helena said when they were alone.

"Don't even know the meaning of the word," he shrugged. "I'm just smiling because I'm glad to see you, Helena. You look good enough to eat."

"Spare me the vulgar metaphors, Mr. Porter."

"Yes, I'm vulgar," he said. "And possessive and passionate too. You share at least those last two traits, Mrs. Swann."

"Really, Sam, no banter today. I wouldn't be able to enjoy it. There's something serious we have to talk about. I just incurred Brad's displeasure to stay behind and tell you."

Shoo-fly sat up straight and flexed his shoulders to relieve his tired back muscles. He listened carefully while she told him about Brunetti and the bribe. His eyes were fixed on her mouth as she spoke.

"Helena, what would a P.I. from Las Vegas want with me? A bribe for what?"

"Don't be coy, Sam. It has to be casino fraud. I found out you were a dealer in Las Vegas."

"He said it was casino fraud?"

"No, but when Mickey told me you were a dealer, I began to put two and two together."

"Oh, sure, your date with Mickey!"

"It was hardly a date. You've spoken to him, haven't you?"

"Yes. But let's get back to Brunetti. How does he figure I can raise thirty thousand dollars?"

"Isn't that obvious? Look, I've been going crazy thinking about it. Now it's your turn. Are you going to tell Angela?"

"Not if I don't have to. Does Brad know?"

"Only you and I know."

"Good. Thank you for that. I'll take care of it."

Helena stared at him, eyebrows raised, expecting more. But he stood up and walked off alone to one of the spare bedrooms. After closing the door and opening the blinds to admit the afternoon sun, he took off his shoes and lay down, hands behind his head. He stared at the coffered ceiling and thought hard about Pedro Brunetti and Wanda Buckley.

CHAPTER 28

STICK TO THE PLAN

WHEN HE FIRST CAME TO TOWN, Mickey Cullion bought a used car right off the street in the Mission District for seven hundred bucks. It was a piece of crap, just like the one he got rid of in Vegas. He figured it was better than walking everywhere, but it seems a car isn't always real convenient in a hilly town like San Francisco. Especially a bomber that tends to stall out on steep inclines. The result being that day to day this wasn't looking like the smartest deal he ever made. Still, he'd need the thing to disappear someday soon. And it came in handy on days off when he wanted a change of scenery.

Like the day Sam planned to have his talk with Wanda Buckley. It was a workday, but Mickey took it off. Sam was fine with that—wasn't going to need him until evening. Mickey intended to head south at first, but thought better about it when he noticed his gas gauge was hovering near empty.

Instead, he took a cable car from Market Street to Fisherman's Wharf, figuring to board the Blue & Gold ferry there for the Alcatraz tour. Then he stopped to think. What the hell did he want to look at an old penitentiary for? Shit, he knew that life and totally hated it. So much for San Francisco's most popular tourist attraction. Chalk up another reason why this town was not his cup of tequila.

A different Blue & Gold ferry was going to a place out in the bay called Angel Island. Now that made more sense. Scenery and fresh air. Lots of hiking trails. It didn't compare to Teton Valley in Idaho where his uncle's cabin was, although it reminded him of the life there—simple and clean, and away from just about everything you put up with in cities.

After killing a couple of hours on the island, Mickey caught the return ferry to Fisherman's Wharf. He strolled around the endless concession stands, then walked out to the pier to watch the harbor seals as they honked and clambered over the docks. Since he hadn't eaten breakfast, he scarfed down a burger with fries at Johnny Rocket's before catching the cable car for Market Street. He had enjoyed his day and was mellowed out by the time he met Sam a block away from the hotel where Wanda Buckley and Brunetti were staying.

The afterglow didn't last long. Sam showed up looking great in a dark sport jacket, white silk shirt and slacks. But no disguise.

"What the fuck, Sam! What happened to the old clothes and mustache?"

"I don't need them. Wanda's going to be eating out of the palm of my hand. When I get her pointed in a new direction, Brunetti won't matter. He'll have to follow."

"Jesus, Sam, I don't know. You got the money yet?"

"A little at a time, Mick. I'm taking less than five grand a day to stay under the radar. The checks go to the Prado Hotel address. I'm still renting that room. We'll meet there before we leave town."

"You got a plan for leaving?"

"Not yet. I hope we can get a week more of this."

"Just remember what I said about splitting the money."

"I'm cashing a few checks at a time. Tomorrow we can split what I have so far."

That made him feel better. But why, oh why did Sam always have to spring surprises on him? Stick to the plan was Mickey's motto. At least he brought the cell phones, like he said he would. Mickey memorized the numbers and called him on the spot, just to make sure he had it right.

The hotel was five stories high. The first floor housed the lobby, a small restaurant and a chain drugstore. There was a canopy covering the lobby entrance that extended out onto the sidewalk. A doorman was posted there from early morning until about four-thirty in the afternoon. Mickey had never seen anyone around in the evening hours until about ten or so, when a security guard would be seated just inside. Brunetti's room was on the fourth floor, Wanda was on two.

They knew Brunetti was out. Mickey had called the hotel from a payphone before meeting up with Sam and asked to be put through to the detective's extension. It rang multiple times until the operator cut back in. By now, he and Sam had moved into place across the street from the hotel in the recessed entrance of a jewelry store that had closed for the day. They were talking about when and how to make contact.

"I'm setting my phone to vibrate. Call me if Brunetti comes back. Let it ring twice and hang up."

"Then what?"

"Follow him in and get positioned on his floor. If he comes out of his room, call and let it ring once. That'll give me time to get out of Wanda's room before he can get down to the second floor."

In the unlikely event that Brunetti came back and went directly to Wanda's room before Mickey could follow, Sam would be on his own. Mickey thought that was dangerous, but he said he could handle it.

"Handle it! How in hell you gonna handle it?"

"Look, I don't intend to give Wanda my real name. But if Brunetti comes in, I'll admit who I am—and I'll still pitch the story about the guy in L.A. You know the drill by now."

"You better have details to back it up. Names, places, stuff that'll hold together for a while."

Sam's mouth was a tight line, and his eyes had darkened. Mickey had pushed too far.

"Lay off. I'm telling you I've got it covered."

He took off across the street with that long stride, barely glancing at the traffic as he went, no doubt figuring people would stop for him. Mickey had to admire his guts, but he wondered where his fuckin' head was at.

The street quieted down after Sam disappeared into the hotel. No traffic either direction, no pedestrians. Still, Mickey was uptight and jittery, shifting from foot to foot in the doorway to try and keep his mind from racing.

Ten minutes passed, maybe a little more. Just as Mickey's heart rate was ratcheting down, his cell phone rang. It gave him a helluva jolt. The hairs on his arms and neck pricked up, and he felt his face get hot. *What the hell!* he thought. *My phone ain't supposed to ring.*

It was Sam.

CHAPTER 29

A BOTTLE OF CANADIAN CLUB

LIEUTENANT VIEJO

It was easy for Shoo-fly to talk his way into Wanda Buckley's hotel room. No one paid him any mind in the lobby, and the elevator door stood open as he walked in and pressed the second floor button. When he stepped out onto Wanda's floor, a maid was pushing her cleaning cart down the aisle to the left. He went right, then doubled back as she disappeared into a room.

At Wanda's door he listened for a moment, then knocked. When he heard her foghorn voice call out to ask who it was, he smiled and thought he might actually enjoy having a conversation with the old lady.

"My name is Ralph, Mrs. Buckley," he said, speaking through the door. "Pedro Brunetti asked me to see you with some information I have. It concerns Lana Firewood."

Right away the dead bolt snapped back, and the door opened. Wanda Buckley was standing there, mouth open and eyebrows raised quizzically.

"Pedro sent you?"

"Yes ma'am."

"Come on in," she said, gesturing for him to enter.

Once inside, Shoo-fly quickly noted several things about the room—location of the bathroom, the fire escape platform outside the window, the papers and folders strewn about the bed and table, and the room service tray with a three-quarters-full bottle of Canadian Club.

"Sit down, young man, sit down," she said,

indicating one of the chairs near the window.

"Why isn't Pedro here with you?"

"He's in the Marina district with some kind of lead, Mrs. Buckley. He thought this was too important to wait."

"Well, what is it then?"

"The man you're after is probably in L.A. I used to see him with Lana in the bars, and I happen to know he left for L.A. the night of her murder."

"You're from Las Vegas?"

"That's right."

"What are you doing in San Francisco?" Wanda asked.

"Does that matter?"

"Yeah, I think it does matter," she said. "Who are you, and what do you really know about my Lana?"

Her eyes were probing his, and her features reflected doubt and distrust. Shoo-fly felt his throat constrict. He must be playing this wrong. All of a sudden, he was lost.

"I know she was a fucking slut!" he shouted, standing up from his chair and pulling his hands out of his pockets.

Wanda's jaw dropped and her eyes went to Shoo-fly's right hand, where the knife was. She surprised him then by dropping her head and pitching forward to butt him hard in the stomach. The knife flew out of his hand, and he fell on his ass, his back propped up by the side of the bed.

Reaching back toward the room service tray, Wanda grabbed the bottle of Canadian Club by its neck. When Shoo-fly clambered up from the floor, she made a terrific roundhouse swing with the bottle. But he sidestepped her as the momentum of her effort spun her around. Her back facing him now, he unleashed a powerful kick to the base of her spine.

She went sprawling face first into the carpet. By the time she rolled over, Shoo-fly had picked up the bottle and cracked it over the glass-top dresser right above her head. The liquor went splashing over both of them. He dropped to his knees straddling her, putting all his weight and force into shoving the bottle's jagged edge deep into her neck. Wanda's fat arms came up to claw at him. She tried to scream, but it came out in a muffled bloody gurgle as Shoo-fly drove and twisted the bottle further into her throat.

He had no idea of time elapsing now. The blood had risen inside and his breath came slow and hard. Fire-red spots filled his vision, and a rush of wind howled inside his ears. He had retrieved his knife from the floor and was carving her up, stopping only when he noticed the stains on his trousers.

Like before in Las Vegas, he needed time to calm down. He sat on the bed, panting, looking around him at the papers and file folders, some of them spattered with blood. What might they be? He spotted his cell phone on the floor by the bed where he had fallen. It must have popped out of his sport jacket pocket. Letting it stay there for now, he stood up and headed for the bathroom, removing his jacket and draping it over the shower curtain rod. He scrubbed his hands with care, took a wash cloth and wet it, and began dabbing at the stains on his trousers. When he finished, he flung the wash cloth aside and looked into the mirror, searching his own eyes for . . . something.

With clean hands now, he went back into the room, picked up the cell phone and called Mickey, who answered in a frightened whisper.

"What?"

"Listen, Mick, is Brunetti back?"

"No. What are you doin' calling me?

"You gotta help me with Wanda. She's drunk, she

passed out on me. We'll put her to bed. And she's got all these papers spread around. There may be some stuff from Brunetti we should read."

"Brunetti could come back while I'm up there."

"I need you for five fucking minutes, Mick. Come on. Now."

Before long there was a tentative knock on the door. Shoo-fly opened it and pulled Mickey in. When he saw all the blood and the bottle stuck in Wanda Buckley's throat, Mick went bug-eyed. He threw up right there at the doorway onto the carpet inside.

He had to be surprised when Shoo-fly made his move, that thousand-yard stare of his telling him it was all over. But Mickey got his shiv out fast, like a magician pulling a dove out of his sleeve. Not that it mattered too much with Shoo-fly grabbing his wrist and spinning him around, jamming his hand and the knife back into the door frame, where it stuck. Mickey was pretty much defenseless, held tight and a foot off the floor.

Shoo-fly had his own knife in play now. He yanked it up to the little man's throat from behind, carving him deep from ear to ear, like a farmer takes a pig on the farm. Mickey gagged and went limp as the blood cascaded down his chest. Shoo-fly pulled his arm away and let him drop, satisfied it was over when Mickey's body crumpled to the floor with a thud and the red pool began to spread on the carpet.

He was laughing now, just a chuckle at first, then loud and derisive.

"Hey Mick," he said, "you went down easier than the old lady."

After going through Mickey's pockets, he made another trip to the bathroom, again washing up carefully. Finally, he put his sport jacket back on, combed his hair and left.

CHAPTER 30

SCOTCH TAPE AND KOTEX

MICKEY CULLION'S MIND was a jumble of racing thoughts and condign fear. Just a knife's edge from oblivion, he had to play possum, try to make Sam think he was dead or dying—which wasn't far from the truth. He didn't know how deep the throat wound was, but he knew—and Sam didn't—that his earlobe had nearly been sliced off. That's where most of the bright red blood was from that made Mickey look like a lost cause.

Getting through it was touch and go. He needed to get pressure on that neck wound, but had to lie still while Sam went through his pockets for the cell phone and his wallet. He figured the bastard wanted to make identification difficult for the cops and to confuse them about what happened. Next thing Mickey heard was water running in the bathroom. When that stopped, it seemed to him that Sam began walking aimlessly about the room—probably wiping down everything he had touched. All this while Mickey was bleeding out on the floor. He was in shock and fading fast by the time Sam opened a window and started down the fire escape to the alley below,

Just before exiting, Sam tossed the towel he was using on the floor. That might have saved Mickey's life. He had barely enough energy left to roll over and snag it when Sam was gone. Winding it around his neck, he pulled it snug and made a knot in front. He applied pressure then, but he couldn't say for how long because he passed out.

He lost a helluva lot of blood. When he woke up he was weak as weak tea, feeling dizzy and sick every time he raised his head. But he goaded himself to concentrate. Getting away was important—he only had to look at poor Wanda to know he couldn't stick around. He was accessory before the fact on this job just like he was accessory after on the last two. He had nobody to call for help and no money on him. And he couldn't go out looking like he did—clothes soaked with blood and a terrycloth towel around his neck.

He stumbled to Wanda's closet and saw a mannish-looking raincoat of hers that would cover most everything. So what if it buttoned the wrong way? He pulled it on and looked in the bathroom mirror. Mickey wasn't a vain guy, but the sight that confronted him almost made him cry. He was a pasty-faced Van Gogh with terrified eyes.

Laying the raincoat aside, Mickey peeled the bloody towel off his neck and washed up as best he could. He grabbed a fresh towel from the rack over the toilet and applied it carefully—no knot this time. Even though he looked a little more respectable this way, he still needed to keep pressure there. So he tore a sleeve off one of Wanda's blouses and tried to use it like a scarf to hide the towel—tying it behind his neck to secure it.

The ear was still oozing blood. He was dabbing at it with a damp washcloth when he spotted a complimentary Kotex pad on the sample tray by the bathroom sink. Pulling the wrapper off, he taped it over his ear with scotch tape from the desk. Then he drew the raincoat back on, jacked the collar up, combed his hair and checked the mirror one last time. It wasn't pretty, but it would do.

Shivering and weak, he sat on the bed, trying to will himself through the window and down the fire escape. *Christ*, he thought, *I'll never make it, I just don't have the strength.* His eyes kept going back to Wanda with the bottle of Canadian Club she ordered from room service stuck in her throat like that. *What an awful fuckin' sight*, he thought.

Then it hit him—*room service*. He knew room service here was somewhere in the basement level. He also knew the elevator stopped in the basement, where there was a service entrance to the back alley. He'd never make it down the fire escape, but he *could* get to the elevator. If he was lucky, nobody would notice while he made his way down and outside to the alley. Going through the lobby again was not an option—that bellhop he knew might see him.

Mickey came out of Wanda's room and wobbled on unsteady legs to the elevator. When it arrived, he pushed the basement level button and leaned on it. To no avail, as they say. Anyone who has ever been desperate for an elevator to go express knows what happens. Instead of bypassing the lobby, it stopped there—and an old couple started to pile in, dragging a brass luggage trolley behind them.

Mickey said, "Down!" to alert them, and watched them back up with lame smiles and apologies.

Finally, his luck kicked in—nobody was around in the basement, and nobody saw him making his way outside. It was dark in the alley, and he rested there for a minute, just leaning against the building and trying to conserve a little energy.

A second helping of luck was finding a taxi right away. He gave the cabbie his address and stumbled into the back seat. Garish images flashed behind his eyes as he faded into a misty half-sleep peopled by circus acts and waterslides. Cutting through a haze of white noise, he heard a man's voice say something, then grow louder, screaming at him now.

"Hey, buddy, this here's your address. C'mon, wake up!"

Mickey passed a hand over his eyes, trying to clear

the mist.

"Oh man, help me out, will ya? I'm sick and I gotta get up to the third floor here."

"Nah, the fare's eleven bucks. Just gimme the fare."

"Yeah, well if you help me pal, I'll give you twenty. Besides, my money's up there."

The cabbie didn't like it much, but he helped him up the two flights of stairs. Mickey fished some bills out of an envelope in his dresser drawer, paid him, then sat on his bed thinking. He needed rest, he needed medical attention, and most of all he needed to be very careful. Good thing he pried his knife out of the door frame before getting out of Wanda's room. The only comfort he had was knowing nobody would get in his crib without having the point of that thing in front of his face.

CHAPTER 31

A DOG RETURNETH

PEDRO BRUNETTI HADN'T HEARD from Helena Swann in the two days since their meeting. His best guess was that she wouldn't mention the bribe to Brad Styles, but would call her sister in Hawaii. Pedro intended to follow up very shortly.

His immediate concern that day was updating Wanda on the case. He avoided her when he could, but he couldn't avoid telling her Bailey Viejo in Las Vegas was interested in Sam Porter. This was a crucial time for him. He had concluded that Wanda would drop him as soon as Viejo spoke to her. With the police finally interested in Porter, why would she want to keep a P.I. on her payroll? Sooner or later, they'd have a DNA sample to match what was culled from the Las Vegas murder scene. And that would be that, he thought.

So, things had come to a head. Any further good he might extract out of the case would have to come from the Sharples empire—before they realized Sam Porter was more than just a casino thief. Pedro still judged that his risks were small. The money he would receive through Helena Swann was merely a fee in his estimation. Could he lose his license? Well, yes, if either she or Angela Porter were to complain. But why would they do that?

Besides, his lukewarm career as a P.I. was about over. As it says in Proverbs, *A dog returneth to his vomit as a fool returneth to his folly.* He didn't want to spend the rest of his life proving that odious truth.

By ten o'clock that morning, he was surprised that Wanda hadn't called. She always had breakfast around that time and would phone him to see whether he wanted to come along. On days he had something to report, he did. When ten-thirty rolled around, he walked down to the second floor and knocked on her door. No answer. Was she so irritated with him that she went off without calling? With Wanda, you could never tell. Wendy's was just two blocks away, so Pedro strolled over, expecting to find her. When he didn't, he began to feel uneasy. Who was more a creature of habit than Wanda? Where could she be?

Back at the hotel, he dithered in the lobby for twenty minutes or so, hoping to see her ample form stride through the door. At eleven-thirty, he asked the manager to call her. When she didn't answer, Pedro prevailed upon him as Wanda's very concerned employee to accompany him to her room with a key.

He was one step through the door when his eyes took in the ghastly scene. At the same time, his foot hit the sticky mess on the carpet and he skidded through it and fell. As so often happens, the crime scene was compromised by the very first person to get there. The hotel manager retreated into the corridor and flipped open his cell phone to dial 911. Pedro stood up, backed out and closed the door. His embarrassment aside, what had happened in that room? Who in hell could have done that to another human being?

~ ~ ~

The detectives who interviewed Pedro set themselves up in the room adjacent to Wanda's. He had stayed in the corridor by her room until they came, the awful stink of blood-soaked puke clinging to him. After explaining what happened, he was led by a crime scene technician to a bathroom where he took off his soiled suit and deposited it in an evidence bag. They found him a robe to wear, but he refused to be interviewed until he had a change of clothes.

Meanwhile, the manager quietly moved customers in rooms on the murder side of the elevator to other floors. He also erected screens with a "Renovations in Progress" sign to keep people in the other wing from straying into the area.

Pedro understood he was a suspect. As the questioning proceeded, he gave the police as much detail as he could recall about his activities in the last twenty-four hours. If the medical examiner pronounced the time of death earlier than 10:30 p.m., he knew that his presence elsewhere in the city could be verified. After sharing selected details of his investigation, he gave them Bailey Viejo's name to corroborate his story. When they realized that his only certain lead, the phone call, pointed to Sharples Communications, the detectives exchanged glances. He surmised that anytime a case led to the offices of a newspaper, an experienced law officer would feel apprehensive.

Although Sam Porter came to mind when he thought about this new crime scene, Pedro didn't throw his name out as a suspect. After all, he was in Hawaii. He did, however, mention him and Mickey Cullion as two people the Las Vegas police might be interested in questioning. It would be Viejo's job to fill them in on that score. In relating everything he knew about Wanda's habits, he mentioned the bellboy she played cards with. Obviously, that fellow would be in for some tough questioning.

Before they released him, Pedro told the detectives he would be around for a few days in case they needed him. As far as returning to Las Vegas, they asked him to check with them first.

~ ~ ~

Now that his only source of current income had dried up, Pedro would soon be feeling the pinch. A man of very modest savings, he couldn't last a week in an upscale town like San Francisco. He'd have to contact Helena Swann right away for a quick resolution to their business. He had already told her she didn't have much time. An urgent reminder was definitely in order.

For some reason, however, he stalled. Playing their previous conversation over in his mind, he tried to think of any objection or delaying tactic Helena might use. He couldn't pinpoint why he did it, but he drove down to the Marina district and past the Sharples mansion before placing his call. At first, he was just looking for a likely pay phone. Then he decided to make sure she was in town. Perhaps he hoped for a chance encounter. He wasn't sure.

The sight that struck him as he drove past the mansion gates was Sam Porter's new Porsche parked in the circular drive. Shouldn't it be stored in the garage, or at the airport? If Porter was back early from Kauai, the consequences might have been deadly for Wanda Buckley.

Pedro pulled his car over to the curb, and fished out his cell phone. He wasn't adept enough at using one to have any numbers programmed in, so he poked around in his wallet for Viejo's card to find his telephone number. The message he recorded left no doubt that this was urgent.

"Lieutenant, this is Pedro Brunetti. I want you to call as soon as you get this, doesn't matter what time. Wanda Buckley was murdered sometime yesterday and I just found out Sam Porter is back in San Francisco." He had no doubt Viejo would make the connection.

Next, he backtracked to downtown and used a pay phone to call the Sharples residence. Helena Swann picked up after the housekeeper answered.

"Who is this?" she demanded.

"Pedro Brunetti, Mrs. Swann. Please don't speak, just listen. I know they've come home. We need to complete our business no later than eleven-thirty tomorrow morning. I'll call you early to let you know where we'll meet."

Giving her no time to respond, he hung up and stepped away from the phone kiosk. It was a cool, cloudy, moonless night. Somewhere in his notes, Pedro knew he'd have Mickey Cullion's address. Sooner or later, he'd have to check up on that boy.

CHAPTER 32

THE SEWING KIT

FACING THE GRIM REALIZATION that he would have to be his own doctor, Mickey Cullion braced himself against the bathroom sink and looked through his medicine cabinet. One of those little sewing kits caught his eye, the kind you steal from motel rooms along with the samples of shampoo and lotion.

It hurt to laugh, but he cracked up at the beige thread. *Might as well have flesh tone stitches*, he thought.

Figuring to sterilize the needle, he ran the hot water. His hands shook while he tried to thread the little hole and tie a knot. Beads of cold sweat stippled his face and drained into his eyes. Holding his head up high in front of the mirror to see what he was doing, he watched his neck wound open up like a pair of long, nasty lips.

The first push of the needle into the skin at his neck was a motherfucker, but after tugging it through, he knew he'd get it done somehow. Spacing the stitches as close together as possible, he lost count after twenty.

That should have been the worst, but no. After resting on the edge of the bathtub for a minute, he inhaled, twisted the cap off a bottle of denatured alcohol, soaked a washcloth with it and pushed it up against the raw, stitched flesh. He wept and choked and slid down into the tub, wailing like he had just lost his mother.

When he stopped coughing and wiped the tears and

sweat away, Mickey thought about getting some sleep. Where, though? Hiding out in his car was one possibility to stay under the radar. But he figured Sam wouldn't be looking for no dead man. Not tonight, anyway. So he remained in the apartment and crashed into his unmade bed. He had never been tired like this. Total weakness. He wasn't even sure he would live.

In the morning, he woke up with pains everywhere—headache, backache, assache. It helped his concentration that he was mad by now. He decided on calling Helena Swann to tell her she and her fuck buddy Sam were going to come up with the money he needed to get away and stay away. First, though, he had to look good enough to go outside.

The ear couldn't be hidden completely, but he could exchange the freaky Kotex and scotch tape bandage for a neat covering of gauze and surgical tape. He'd need some gauze at his neck too, but maybe he could hide it with a black rayon scarf he had. That, and a button-down white shirt open at the collar. It was kind of retro, like a beatnik might have worn back in the fifties, especially with a beret—not that you'd ever see him in one of those.

After making the call to Helena, Mickey would have to live in his car until he had some money. Otherwise, Sam would show up and try to finish the job he started. Nobody at work had seen his car, including Sam, and his neighbors didn't know him. He'd be safe there for a while if he played it smart.

He was hungry, which meant he was getting better, didn't it? Needing to be seen as little as possible, he couldn't go out to a restaurant. So he put two biscuits of Shredded Wheat in a bowl and poured in milk and sugar. That would have to do. With his neck swollen and throbbing, though, he could barely swallow. In disgust, he flipped the cereal into the sink and just sipped the milk. Maybe tomorrow he could eat.

As soon the morning rush hour had cleared, he walked three blocks to a drugstore to use a payphone. Last night's cell phone was long gone—Sam probably took it. The few people he saw on the street seemed to be staring. Was he paranoid? Most likely, they could see he didn't have his sea legs.

Helena Swann answered on the first ring. She sounded awfully pissed off when he asked for money.

"If you want money, call him directly. He's not here and I certainly won't talk to you."

"You hang up and you'll be the sorriest socialite bitch in San Francisco," he said. "I know enough about you and Sam to make problems. Now you gonna listen?"

The ice in her voice turned to sweet reason.

"Why don't you call Sam at the office, Mickey. You know I don't have any money of my own."

"It's better for me to get you involved. I don't wanna see him. He tried to hurt me last night. That wicked temper of his, you know? Call him for the money he owes me—he knows exactly how much—and tell him I want *you* to deliver it in a big envelope to my address. If he shows up, it's all over."

"Give me your phone number," she demanded.

Already trying to nail him. Mickey shook his head and sighed.

"For chrissake, shut up and listen," he said. "There's a little lobby inside the front entrance to my place. Just leave the money in an envelope with my name on it under the mailboxes. I'll pick it up when I see you leave. Don't come upstairs, I won't answer the door."

"How can we reach you?"

"You can't. Don't try. And the money has to be there by tomorrow morning at ten o'clock. Any later I'll be gone, and I guarantee Sam has trouble."

"What if I need to see you with a message? How do I know Sam will just send the money without conditions?"

"Fuck Sam and any conditions. Pardon my French . . . Helena. Tell you what, you want to see me, come in broad daylight between nine and ten tomorrow morning and stand at the front door for a full five minutes holding the envelope. I'll find a way to signal you."

What she didn't know was that he wouldn't be looking down from some window, he'd be a whole block away on a cross street where he could see the entrance from his car. If she did wait the five minutes, what the hell, he'd drive over and pick her up.

On his way to the payphone, he had ditched everything he took from Wanda's room—raincoat, blouse sleeve, and Kotex pad. Walking back to his place, he wondered if someone had found her yet and how much time it would be before the cops made a connection to Sam. And something new was starting to bother him—Brunetti. The private dick would be the first one the police turned to when the body was discovered. Which meant Mickey's name would be coughed up as well as Sam's.

Shit, he thought. *This is gonna be close.*

CHAPTER 33

HUSH MONEY

HELENA SWANN WAS INCENSED. That vulgar little worm was incredibly sure of himself, she thought, demanding money, threatening to reveal her affair with Sam. He could never prove anything, of course, but a scandal would ruin her.

Sam laughed when she called him at work about Mickey.

"Helena, what is this?" he said. "I'm supposed to believe Mickey called you for money this morning?"

"Why would I lie about such a thing? He wants the money you owe him—he says you know exactly how much. And he won't deal with you because you hurt him last night."

Sam was silent. For a moment Helena thought the line was dead.

"What happened last night?" she asked. "What did you do?"

"Listen, I don't want to talk about it now. I admit pushing him around, but I didn't think it was that serious. He didn't show up at work today. I'll just have to go see him, that's all."

"He said it's all over if you show up. He seemed to be threatening me with disclosure and you with police trouble."

"Helena, it's just a nuisance thing. He knew I was going to fire him. Tell me exactly what he wants. It might be worth it to get rid of him."

When she told him, he seemed appreciative that she was willing to go to Mickey's place with the money.

"You know, I really did knock him around too

147

much. But if you can talk to him a minute when you get there, we could be sure he'd just go away and be quiet about this."

"How?"

"By reminding him how well I know him. By looking at him straight in the eye as only you can and telling him you know he's involved with *everything* I did in Las Vegas. Simple as that, Helena."

"Does that mean Brunetti is after him as well as you?"

"Absolutely."

"I wouldn't mind putting the little creep in his place after the way he spoke to me today."

"Then do it. For me . . . and for you."

After saying she would, Angela wondered how in the world she had gotten herself even more tangled up in Sam's affairs. And it occurred to her that he had never mentioned taking care of the situation with Pedro Brunetti.

That evening was when Brunetti called with his ultimatum. So now there were *two* low rent characters expecting her to act as bag woman for their hush money. Helena was beyond angry—she wouldn't do it alone, Angela had to be pulled into it now. Maybe she wouldn't have to know about Mickey, but someone other than Helena was going to have to meet with Brunetti.

Finding Sam and Angela in the library, something odd struck her about the scene. Angela was sitting in an overstuffed tapestry armchair, reading a magazine. Sam stood across the room, one big, hairy arm supporting the other, a drink in his right hand. He was dressed in black gabardine slacks and a black polo shirt with a thin red line across the chest. He seemed to be staring at Angela, and Helena thought his demeanor somehow menacing. For the first time, she realized he had no real feeling for his wife, probably didn't even like her very much.

CHAPTER 34

CASINO FRAUD?

ANGELA'S BEAUTIFUL WORLD began to fall apart that night. When her sister rushed into the library, Angela was reading the New York Review of Books—a thing Sam was condescending about, as if she were some airhead with intellectual pretensions. That was the latest, nagging sign something was amiss between them. It frightened her to think that their relationship ended at physical fulfillment.

At first, she couldn't make sense out of the things Helena was saying about a bribe to be paid and Sam under suspicion of casino fraud in Las Vegas. Despite Helena's increasing agitation, he grew more and more quiet and self-contained.

"Sam, please . . . what is this?" Angela asked.

Slowly, he put his drink down and contemplated it a moment, before turning a baleful glance at Helena. While the sisters waited, he seemed to be drawing energy from a secret source. When he spoke, his tone was calm, almost philosophical. Angela received the impression he was happy to get this off his mind.

"Helena's telling the truth, darling. It must be very hard for her to come in here like this. She's known for a couple of days and has been good enough not to bother you or Brad with it. In Las Vegas, I was a dealer at the Riviera and . . . I fell in with a friend who had a plan to skim small amounts of money, something we could execute every day. When my uncle died and I had a little money ahead, I called the scam off. Somehow this investigator has found out about it and thinks he can blackmail me. I wouldn't be worth his trouble, I'm sure, except for your position and the Sharples name."

"Sam, I can hardly believe this!"

"I don't even mind admitting it, Angela, except for the stupidity of it. That, and facing your disappointment in me."

All she wanted now was to protect him, shelter him from his own venality. He had come so far in such a short time, making his mark in her organization with no push or help from her. Surely this was an aberration that they could get past. She rose out of the chair and went to him, threw her arms around him and wept.

"That's the second time I've made you cry, Angela," he said, smiling now and holding her chin up. "Do you remember the first?"

"Of course I do," she murmured.

"Well, we just won't pay him," he said. "I'll stay home tomorrow and when he calls, I'll tell him there's no deal. You and Brad will have my resignation effective immediately. I'm a consultant after all, not an employee of Sharples. Maybe the publicity can be confined to Las Vegas when I'm indicted there."

"Sam, no. I can't begin to think of that. Thirty thousand isn't really a lot of money. Unless you think he'll keep coming back."

"Hard to say. But he has something to lose, too. He could be arrested for concealing and abetting the fraud if we turn him in. No, he'll probably stay away after this."

"Then we should pay him. I'll get the money tomorrow."

"You'll do this for me, Angela?"

"You know I'd do anything for you," she said. "I'll take my cell phone with me to the bank and Helena can tell me where to meet him when he calls here."

"Better if Helena can call him now and tell him what will happen."

"Yes, I can do that," Helena said. "I'll leave a message that Angela will meet him, not me."

"Right," he said. "That way he won't be surprised tomorrow, and Helena can stay out of it. The landline here will forward to your cell phone, Angela. Just call me as soon as you can afterwards. We'll meet in town."

While they worked this through, Helena seemed agitated.

"It's just not that simple," she said. "You won't be able to go on as before. This fellow was very clear that the police might be following up. The thirty thousand will only give us time—and a report on his evidence that might help us decide what to do."

Angela was baffled. "What are you saying?" she said.

"She's saying I may want to . . . disappear after you have the report. Is that it, Helena?"

"That's possible. He's supposed to tell us the exact charges and the evidence he has to support it. But he's so cagey, I'm worried."

"Sounds to me like he may pull a surprise."

"That's what I'm afraid of," Helena said.

Angela was frowning and wringing her hands.

"What surprise?" she asked, looking to each of them.

"I don't know," Helena said. "But it seems to me Brunetti feels he can walk away from this and we'll have no recourse. Something he knows makes him confident we won't expose him as a blackmailer."

Angela was so rattled she became physically ill. Sam helped her to bed and stayed with her until the sleeping pill kicked in. But she knew what she had to do. She would save her husband. No matter what happened, they could fight it, and she would bring him back home.

CHAPTER 35

GALLOWS HUMOR

WHAT A PERFORMANCE, Helena thought. As someone who had manipulated people all her life, she knew the mark of the master when she saw it. Sam was so good, she was mesmerized. She stayed on in the library when he and Angela went upstairs, wondering how it would play out.

Around nine-thirty, she went to the kitchen and heated water for tea. Despite the dangers piling up around them, she felt a renewed sense of living large. There was something calming about seeing a path ahead, believing that she and Sam could challenge these obstacles and win. In less than half an hour, he joined her, sitting by her side at the kitchen island. The usual sardonic smile was gone, the mocking eyes extinguished.

"How is Angela?" she asked.

"Sleeping. She took a pill. I sat with her until she dozed off."

"I hope she's up to this. She has never had to do anything remotely unethical or illegal, you know."

Sam ignored this and stared at her a moment. He rested his hands on his knees.

"Are you with me in this, Helena? Even if you can't come away with me now, will you wait for me? Somehow I'll work out a way for us to be together."

She thought of Brad first, however briefly, then slid off the stool to her knees and hugged Sam around the waist, nestling her cheek against his inner thigh. He took a handful of hair and slowly raised up her head to search her face. His eyes had grown dark and moody, his expression was feral and possessive. She could feel his manhood rise hard between her breasts.

There's a kind of gallows humor in making love with the law closing in, something of the licentiousness of plague victims in the Middle Ages who rutted in the streets in full view of a frightened populace. Who, after all, would stop them? For two people having an affair, Helena and Sam hadn't many opportunities to make love before this. And certainly they hadn't ever given free rein to their need for one another until this evening. They raced to her room on the second floor. Their passion was enhanced knowing that his wife—her sister—was sleeping only a few doors away in the conjugal bed.

The exemplary wife who would gladly raise thirty thousand for him was being cuckolded by the step-sister who couldn't raise a dime, but who wanted him enough to risk her own future for a night of unbridled sex. And still Helena thought she might back away from him at the opportune moment and salvage her engagement to Brad. Brad, who couldn't excite her but could provide for and love her.

As before, Sam was part savage, part tender lover. Helena was equally possessed, by turns maternal and caressing, then clawing and demonic. At dawn, they lay in her bed, exhausted. Sam was on his back, one foot on the floor and his hands behind his head. She was stretched out close beside him, on her side with one arm flung across his chest. Scanning his face in profile, she could see he was far away into his thoughts.

"You'd probably best go to Angela now," she said.

He stirred and looked at her absently.

"M-m-m, you're right. I'll go. Thanks for this."

He got out of bed and walked to the chair where he had neatly hung his trousers, putting them on as well as a white tank top t-shirt, the type people call a wife-beater. He turned to her and smiled cautiously, polo shirt draped across his arm, shoes and socks clutched in his right hand.

"Sam?" she said.

"Yes?"

"You don't love Angela, do you? Not even a little."

"No more than you love Brad, Helena Troia."

"Oh, my feelings for Brad. Not a grand passion, but I do love him."

"Like a brother maybe?"

"A little more, I think. Have you ever loved someone, Sam?"

"I loved my mother until I figured out she was a whore. Then I hated her and left home. Maybe I don't know what love is. But I can feel deeply. And I can turn my heart to stone when someone crosses me."

Angela felt a tingle of alarm.

"Why do you say that now?" she asked.

"I didn't just push Mickey around yesterday. I tried to kill him. He crossed me once too often."

"But he worships you! How could you want to kill him?"

"He gave a cop and Brunetti my name in Vegas. That's one reason. His date with you is the other."

"I asked *him* to meet with me! He never touched me."

"He should have said no. I don't trust *anybody* around you."

She was flabbergasted. His intensity was disturbing, and she was repelled but curious, wondering how anyone's deepest feelings could be so hateful.

"How am I going to meet with him now, Sam?"

"It should be easier now, Helena. You wanted to put him in his place, remember? Wasn't it you called him a little creep? I know you can show him who's boss. You're great at it."

It was evident he thought her his equal in some ways. But they were his most evil ways. And this murderous impulse with Mickey was beyond stupid, it was careless.

She erupted. It was fear and anger speaking all at once.

"So you bungle the job with Mickey and I have to clean it up? What next? Do you want me to kill him for you?"

"Now there's an idea. But watch out, he's very good with a knife."

Sam was at the door now, ready to walk away. But not before grinning at her salaciously. If she could have reached him, she would have slapped his face.

~ ~ ~

The three of them ate breakfast together at six-thirty. Sam sat very close to Angela and held her hand the entire time. It was the right thing to do, of course, but it galled Helena. Esther served fruit cup, eggs, sausage and home fries with toast. Sam ate like a wolf while Angela could only manage a cup of tea with lemon. Helena had a fruit cup and coffee.

Angela looked pale and vulnerable, yet it made her appear more attractive and luminous than ever. How Helena loved her for herself and hated her for everything she had, everything wonderful that was always just handed to her. But she did have a grip on the one thing that meant something to her sister—Sam. The only evil thing Angela ever touched or desired, and it was Helena's for the taking.

Whether she wanted it or not was an open question. Why did she keep getting caught up in his machinations? If he got away, how would he live? On Angela's money, of course. Did he think they could both live on her? Certainly not if she knew. But did she have to? Helena had to give it up for the moment. She couldn't keep thinking like this and get through the day.

Sam left as soon as he finished eating. He had to get the money he owed Mickey and deliver it to her. It was at the Prado Hotel where he still rented a room.

"Angela, baby, I have to get to work early," he said. "Brunetti will want to see you alone, so I can't be with you. Are you going to be all right?"

"Yes, I think so," she said. "The bank opens at nine. I'll call you both when it's . . . over. Will you be staying home, Helena?" she asked.

"I'm supposed to meet Hilary Saunders around nine," she lied. "But call my cell phone anytime."

Sam phoned from Sharples Communications at eight-thirty. He agreed to be on a street corner two blocks away from the Tremont building, where Helena could drive up and get the package at nine. She still couldn't decide whether she would try to speak to Mickey or just deliver the envelope. Esther brought in the newspaper as she was leaving, and Helena noticed that Wanda Buckley had been found murdered in a downtown hotel room. She didn't have time to read the story, but she wondered what in the world Wanda was doing in San Francisco.

CHAPTER 36

A FRIENDLY MEETING

LIEUTENANT VIEJO

MY CONTACT IN SAN FRANCISCO homicide was Detective Maynard Bennett. I called him right after Brunetti let me know Sam Porter was in town and Wanda Buckley had been murdered. Brunetti didn't say whether he thought the two events were connected. But if there's one thing about a P.I. you can bet on, it's that he's no longer interested in a case when the customer croaks—foul play or no.

Detective Bennett's partner was Detective Sergeant Alfonso Bowers. Bennett was a tall, rugged, bald guy with a surprisingly soft voice and deferential manner. Al Bowers was a slim, well-groomed black man of average height, gruff in manner, cautious and intelligent. I took the early flight from Las Vegas and met with them at 850 Bryant St. as soon as they had finished interrogating the bellboy for the second time.

Bowers spoke first. "What can we do for you, Viejo?"

"Well, I thought this was just going to be a courtesy call, until I heard Wanda Buckley was dead. I've been authorized to come to San Francisco to tail a suspect who may have left his DNA at the scene of two murders in Las Vegas. Pedro Brunetti has probably made you aware that this occurred in Wanda's home."

"Do you think there's a connection between our cases?" Bennett asked.

"I don't know, but it seems to me we should explore it."

"If we didn't have a very good suspect, I might be inclined to agree," Bowers said.

In order to encourage their full cooperation, I was the first to lay my cards on the table. I told them the story of Sam Porter and Mickey Cullion as far as we knew it. There was no direct evidence, but a DNA sample might tie one of them to the scene and to the murder weapon. I also told them the story of the phone call, which tied someone in San Francisco to the case. Naturally, Brunetti had disclosed this in describing his investigation.

"Lieutenant Viejo," said Bennett, "I don't like the bellhop for the Buckley murder and Al here knows it. But I think the kid will cop to it if we press him. The best thing he could do right now is lawyer up."

This was Bennett's way of giving me a way in to their case and their thinking. I took it up immediately. From the look on Bowers' face, I knew he'd have something harsh to say to Bennett later.

"Look," I said. "We all know that a confession to a murder can close a case down as far as any other leads are concerned. Which is fine if you have concrete evidence. But if you did, you'd both still be pressing the kid for that confession and not talking to me. What's holding you up?"

Bowers sighed and ran his hand across his forehead.

"Viejo, the crime scene techs aren't finished, but we know there's a hell of a lot of blood at the scene doesn't match the vic or the bellboy. Different blood type entirely. There's also vomitus at the scene needs DNA testing, but is unlikely to match up with Buckley."

"So you think a second body was moved for some reason?" I asked.

"Maybe," Bennett said. "Or a second vic might have walked. Or Wanda Buckley might have done a number on her killer before he got away. We don't know."

"Look, we both have DNA samples that need to be checked out. And there are connections, even if they seem pretty indirect, to Sam Porter and his sister-in-law. Leaving Mickey Cullion out of the mix for now, don't you think you could get a warrant out of this from a friendly judge?"

I didn't need to ask Bennett his opinion. We both looked at Bowers. He stared back with a rueful expression, apparently weighing a weak sure thing against a strong hunch built on coincidence. If the tables had been turned, I knew I wouldn't have liked the choice either.

"Okay, okay, I give up. Before Bennett starts the paperwork, tell us where Porter lives and what he's been doing in San Francisco as far as you know."

I wasn't very far into my story before they understood that Shoo-fly worked for Sharples Communications and was married to Angela Sharples. They both sat back in their chairs and looked at each other wide-eyed.

"Kee-rist!" said Bennett. "I was wondering why the name Porter rang a bell."

"Viejo," said Bowers, "do you fucking realize you're asking us to serve paper on the husband of a woman with connections to everybody in the power structure of San Francisco?"

Suddenly, the bellboy was looking real good again to my new pals. The warrant was out for now. But a friendly meeting would be arranged with Mr. Porter. If he would see us at his office without counsel, I could tag along.

At this point, I had no standing in their case. No connection was admitted, and I would have to stay in the background. Having no choice, I agreed. Bowers called Sharples Communications and spoke directly to

Shoo-fly. Citing a crushing workload, he asked Bowers to state his business so he could clarify matters at once. Bowers demurred, saying only that the investigation concerned him and several others and couldn't be handled over the telephone. Shoo-fly claimed he wanted to help but could only spare a half-hour if we came right away. Bowers told him that would be fine.

"Ground rules, Viejo," Bowers said when he got off the phone. "I'll introduce myself to Mr. Porter as San Francisco homicide. When I introduce you and Bennett, you'll flash your badges, and I'll say you're my colleagues. That will be the truth. If you have a few questions that haven't been answered by the end of the interview, ask them. But make sure you stay away from the Las Vegas murders. Not our jurisdiction."

~ ~ ~

When I finally met Shoo-fly, I was surprised. He was bigger, better looking, and smoother than I had imagined. He was wearing a dark blue summer weight wool suit with a gray buttoned-down shirt and a silk tie with alternating bands of violet and gold and rows of light blue flowers. His black hair was neatly trimmed and combed back from his forehead. He was talking to someone on the phone when we arrived, but he smiled brightly and waved us into his office.

I asked myself how this man could have a history that included prizefighting, work as a ranch hand, bartender, bouncer and casino dealer. Behind the GQ good looks, however, I did notice the powerful physique. And even big-shot executives don't look *that* sure of themselves when three homicide detectives walk in. This was a con man, I was sure of it.

After Bowers handled the introductions, we sat around a small, round conference table that took up one side of the office.

"Gentlemen," said Shoo-fly, "I need to see my boss

at ten-thirty. Let's take care of this quickly so I can get out of here by ten twenty-five."

"Certainly, Mr. Porter," Bowers said. "We're investigating the murder of Wanda Buckley, a woman from Las Vegas who has been in San Francisco a short time."

He paused a moment to see if Shoo-fly would volunteer anything. But he only smiled and looked as if he were mystified.

"Do you know Wanda Buckley, Mr. Porter?"

"Detective Bowers, I worked in Las Vegas for a while. Wanda Buckley is . . . or was . . . a well-known real estate agent there. But I never knew her."

"Do you know a man named Michael Cullion?"

"Of course I know Mickey. He worked for me here until he failed to show up for the last two days. He's been terminated."

"For a two-day absence?" asked Bennett.

"Yes, he failed to call, and we haven't been able to contact him. New employees at Sharples are on probation for three months, and any unexcused absence is cause for termination."

"How long have you known Mr. Cullion?" Bowers asked.

"Do you think Mickey had something to do with Wanda Buckley's murder?"

"Please, Mr. Porter, how long have you known him?"

"Oh, I don't know exactly, around five years, I guess."

"Does he have a history of prior arrests that you know of?"

"Gentlemen, this makes me uncomfortable. Hadn't you better talk to him about that?"

"We'll do that, Mr. Porter. Would you give us his address?"

"Sorry, I can't give out an employee address. You'll have to check with Human Resources."

Bowers nodded. "Sure. How about you Mr. Porter, any priors you care to tell us about?"

Shoo-fly laughed. It was a pretty good strategy, and he had a nice way of admitting his prison term, which we already knew about.

"Fellas, I was a prizefighter in Tucson for about a year. That was over ten years ago, but I gained a reputation and carried my boxing prowess into the bars afterwards. My background was pretty rough and tumble until I served that stretch for fighting—felonious assault, they called it. I got straightened out then, and I haven't been in trouble since. I have a college degree from credits I earned in prison."

"We understand, Mr. Porter. We're just trying to corroborate connections we're aware of between you and Mr. Cullion. We know you were in prison together. Did you stay in touch with him while you and your wife were in Hawaii?"

"I called him once on business. I wanted to know if he had delivered certain reports I'm responsible for."

"I see. What day and what time did you return from Hawaii, sir?"

"It was three days ago. We got in about nine o'clock Monday morning at San Francisco airport."

"Uh-huh. Tell us where you were and your activities Tuesday afternoon and evening."

I thought what Shoo-fly did next was damn clever. He paused a moment as if recollecting. An apprehensive look came over him—as if he suddenly realized these cops might suspect him of murder. Finally, he tightened his lips, looking at each of us in turn to show us he was offended at the very thought of it. I was absolutely sure that Bowers and Bennett caught all this and were already discounting him as a suspect.

"I was at work until five on Tuesday. I went directly home after that. I had dinner with my wife and sister-in-law, and we stayed home all night."

"You didn't go out at all?"

"No, I didn't. Is that it, gents? Can I go now?"

I piped up before Bowers could agree to call it a day.

"Mr. Porter, when you first came to San Francisco from Las Vegas, Helena Swann was also on the airline passenger manifest. I understand she's your sister-in-law. Did you know her at the time?"

Shoo-fly looked at me very intently, as if he sensed something was happening that wasn't in the script. Al Bowers sat up straight and cocked his head. His look was a warning to me.

"Interesting question, Detective . . . what is your name?"

"Viejo. Pronounced vyay-ho, but spelled V-I-E-J-O."

He continued to stare.

"I was in first class on that flight, and Helena was in economy class. We met in the airport."

"Just to clarify that, you didn't know her before you met in the airport?"

"Correct," he said.

His tone was quiet, and he kept staring. I had the feeling that comes over you when a storm is gathering, and the sky grows dark.

"You know, Mr. Porter, a private detective Wanda Buckley hired told us he called your boss to ask about something that happened in Las Vegas around the time you first came here. Did Mr. Styles ever discuss this with you?"

"No. Does it concern me?"

"I don't know. This P.I. was trying to trace a call made from Sharples Communications to Wanda

Buckley a couple of hours after two people were murdered in her home."

"Seems to me I recall the case from the newspaper accounts. Are you investigating a Las Vegas murder, Detective Viejo? Wouldn't that be out of your jurisdiction?"

"The P.I. was here in San Francisco with Wanda Buckley, and his statement included this information. We just wanted to ask about it since you were good enough to give us some time."

"I see. But I don't know anything about it. Well, is that it? I really have to go now."

Shoo-fly stood up while we left. He smiled and nodded at Bowers and Bennett. Just before stepping out of his office, I turned to look back at him. He was glaring at me openly, mouth twisted and nostrils flaring. As we made eye contact, my flesh tingled. He knew I knew something and wanted to let me know he didn't give a shit.

Al Bowers gave me a pretty good look of his own when we walked out through the lobby of the Tremont building.

CHAPTER 37

THE ESCORT

BRAD STYLES WAS AT WORK when Angela called him from the bank. At first, he couldn't quite understand her. Was she crying? Apparently, the manager was insisting she have an escort to leave because she had just made a large withdrawal in cash.

"I can be there in ten minutes, Angela," he said. "Where is Sam?"

"He left for work very early, Brad, and I know he's extremely busy, so I thought of you."

"Glad to help, Angela. Listen, I won't ask you to tell me over the phone, but you might let me know what this is about when I get there."

"Oh . . . sure Brad."

She sounded dismayed, but he could hardly fail to ask why she needed to make a withdrawal of that size. Did Sam know about this?

Things didn't get better anytime soon. First, he was held up in traffic. When he finally reached the bank fifteen minutes later, Angela was a trembling wreck. Her chin quivered and she could hardly look him in the eye.

He signaled to the bank manager. When he came over to them, Brad asked for the use of an office where Angela and he could talk freely. The manager led them to the safe deposit area and ushered them into one of the small rooms where patrons can examine the contents of their boxes. There were two chairs in the room and a counter across the back wall. The floor space was no larger than seven by six feet. Angela was holding on tightly to a large manila envelope.

"Angela, there's no reason to be afraid now," he said as gently as possible, "just tell me what's going on."

"Brad, I don't think I should."

"Why, Angela? Did you promise not to tell anyone?"

"Well, no. I just know Sam wouldn't want you to know. You're his boss, after all."

"I may be his boss, but my whole work life revolves around taking care of your business, Angela. Please tell me about this."

She had managed to hold back the tears until that moment. It made him sick to watch this wonderful woman weep over some awful problem that was out of her control.

"Brad, we're being blackmailed."

"Who, Angela, you and I, the company?"

"No, Sam and I."

"Sam knows about this, your coming here? How could he not be with you?"

She didn't answer. He was growing angry and trying not to show it.

"Angela, please help me out. Who is doing this to you and why?"

"A private detective called Helena to demand thirty-thousand dollars so he wouldn't report certain information to his client. It's about Sam and something that happened in Las Vegas."

Transfixed, Brad was listening to a litany made of the clues he had brooded over for weeks. *Sam, Helena, Las Vegas, a private investigator.* But it was the thought of Helena's involvement that gnawed at him. What could it possibly mean?

"Why didn't this man call you or Sam? Why Helena?"

"She was the one who took the call, Brad. Sam and I were on our honeymoon at the time."

"I see. What information does he have on Sam?"

"Well, we think it must be about casino fraud. Sam was part of a scheme there for a while."

"Is the bribe supposed to keep the charges from becoming public, Angela?"

"The bribe won't stop anything, but will give us time. The detective will tell us exactly what he knows and that may help us. Sam may have to . . . get out of town, Brad."

"If Sam won't face this, why doesn't he run now? Why pay a blackmailer?"

"Oh, Brad, all I know is this Brunetti person will hide his evidence. But he won't guarantee somebody else doesn't dig it up like he did."

There was the name—Pedro Brunetti—the Las Vegas P.I. who called him, then wouldn't talk.

"Angela, I want you to be strong about this. The best way to help Sam is to tell this crook we won't do business with him. I can't condone Sam's avoiding the law and running, but that's up to you and him. Either way, this detective won't help. He'll be back for more or he'll sell the same information to the casino. You can't win this way."

"He should call me any time now."

"This person has your cell phone number?"

"It will forward from home, Brad. He'll be calling to tell me where to meet him."

"Well, you *won't* meet him. I'll take your phone right now, Angela. And that envelope. If he calls, he'll meet with me or with no one. But there'll be no hush money. This stops now."

It took a while to convince her, but Brad prevailed when she came to believe it was in Sam's best interest to stay and fight the charges. She was at pains to assure him Sam had offered to return to Las Vegas to avoid publicity in San Francisco, but Brad had to wonder if he had been sincere. Nevertheless, she was calm enough now to drive herself home. He told her not to speak to Helena or Sam, that he would deliver the news to both of them.

Back in his office, Brad turned it over in his mind, then asked his assistant to help him with a confidential project.

"Linda, I want a report by project cost center on Sam Porter. All the hours he has worked since we hired him should be included. And give me the same kind of report on Michael Cullion."

"Michael Cullion has been terminated, Mr. Styles."

"Really? I didn't know. Still, I want the report."

"Yes, sir."

"And one more thing, Linda. A report on the fund we set up for Mr. Porter's project. I want to look at all disbursements by line item."

When Linda left his office, Brad sat back in his chair and stared out the window. He had led this organization for many years at what he thought was a very high standard. What kind of scandal was about to erupt now? Could it be contained? He wondered what he would say when Brunetti called. But his thoughts kept returning to his fiancée. Helena had known about this for days and had chosen to tell him nothing. Why on earth would she do that?

Looking for something to relieve the tension, he glanced at the newspaper to finish the story about Wanda Buckley's murder. He had started reading it earlier when Angela interrupted. Towards the end of the article, he noticed a quote from . . . *Pedro Brunetti*. His jaw dropped. He had to be dreaming. He just had to be!

CHAPTER 38

DO NOTHING RASH

NOT WANTING TO LEAVE her car anywhere in the Mission district, Helena found a parking lot a few blocks away and walked over to the address Mickey had given her. She had pulled her hair back and was dressed in jeans, tank top and sandals. Except for a stainless steel watch, she wore no jewelry, and her makeup was minimal—eyeliner, a little blush, and lipstick. Still feeling conspicuous, she pulled a pair of sunglasses from her bag and put them on.

She wasn't fearful down there, she just didn't like being anywhere near poverty, a condition she was determined never to accept for herself. Most of the people she saw seemed respectable enough. One difference she noticed was that teenagers here looked straight at you instead of pretending you didn't exist, which was one of their more common affectations in her neighborhood.

The building Mickey lived in was a run-down three-story Victorian with all the old trim chopped off, the paint job a monochrome brownish-grayish and badly chipped. Screens to the storm windows were ragged where they still existed. The front door was reached by a crumbling brownstone stoop, and the door itself was badly gouged and covered with footmarks.

It was unlocked. When she walked into the foyer, she had to retreat a step while a disheveled young man pushed past her and down the stairs. She suspected he had been sleeping there on the rotting linoleum tiles among the papers and trash that littered the floor. The inner door was locked. Operated by a buzzer, most likely. She saw the call buttons and mailboxes let into the wall to the right of the door as Mickey had said.

Deciding not to leave the package Sam gave her in such a place, she went back outside to wait until Mickey gave her a signal. Looking up at the windows, she tried to spot him, but no one stirred. Finally, she stood to one side of the front stairs and rummaged in her bag for a cigarette and lighter. It was the first time she had ever smoked on the street.

Cattycorner to the building was a side street with parking on one side. Helena noticed a gray-haired Asian man in a cardigan sweater standing on the corner. He was gesticulating with a knobby cane and raging incoherently at passers-by. Then a decrepit auto with a faded red-turning-orange paint job whizzed around the corner and came to a stop in front of her. It was Mickey, looking gaunt and deathly pale. He was leaning out the window and shouting at her. *What a little beast*, she thought.

"Get in if you wanna talk. Otherwise, come on over and gimme the package."

She hesitated.

"C'mon Helena," he said. "What are you afraid of?"

"Not you, monkey boy," she said, angry now and stepping into the street to get to the passenger side.

"I guess you're good at calling names, Mrs. Swann. I would've thought that was . . . *beneath you*. Did I get that right?"

"Consider it payback for calling me '*one sorry socialite bitch*.' I'm not the only one good at calling names."

As soon as she got in, Mickey pulled out from the curb and into traffic. This was a little disconcerting, but she supposed he didn't want to hang around and discover Sam coming along to trap him.

"Look," he said, "we can do this as fast as you want. You need to say something, say it. But first put the package down between us."

Helena complied.

"How much is in there?" he asked.

"I have no idea. Sam handed it to me just a half hour ago."

Glancing into the back seat, she could see it was littered with clothes, a breakfast cereal carton and some other food items. He had to be living out of this filthy car now, she thought. He must be very afraid. Well, why not use that to her advantage?

"You know, Mickey, revenge is a lousy motivation. I don't know how much Sam put in that envelope or whether you're going to think it's right. But even if it's not what you expect, don't do anything rash."

"What's that supposed to mean?" he said. "I had a rash once, but it cleared up."

She judged him as angry, but very nervous.

"What won't clear up is how Sam feels about you now, Mickey. He wants you to remember that everything that happened in Las Vegas involves the two of you. And he wants you to know that Brunetti has been turned around. He works for us now."

It was easy to tell she had pushed the right buttons. Mickey's breathing was raspy, and he was starting to sweat. His eyes darted over to her from time to time as she spoke. Then he swallowed hard.

"You know what happened in Vegas?" he whined.

"I know everything, Mickey."

"Yeah? You know he tried to kill me!"

"He told me. And all you have to do now is go away and keep quiet. Because anything that brings him down, brings you down."

They were on Market Street now. He pulled over to the curb.

"Okay, that's it, get out of the car."

She opened the door and stepped out, turning back and bending over to speak to him through the window.

"What should I say to Sam for you, Mickey."

"Just that he's got the partner he always wanted now. You're something, lady. See you in hell someday."

CHAPTER 39

UNION SQUARE

PEDRO BRUNETTI TRIED TO THINK logically about where he stood. On the plus side, he was cleared of any suspicion in Wanda's death, and Detective Bennett said he could return to Las Vegas whenever he wanted. Also, he had met with Wanda Buckley's brother, who had arrived in San Francisco to take care of her effects. On that side of the ledger, things were all wrapped up.

But he wasn't at all sure he would go back to Sin City. The town was played out for him, he needed to face that. When he collected his 'fee' from the Sharples clan, he might want to live elsewhere—his old hometown in Mississippi, for instance. He wasn't too proud to put on an apron and work at Home Depot or Wal-Mart for pocket money. Steady work, less hassle. And for the first time in his life, he'd have a little nest egg in the bank.

After retrieving Helena Swann's message from his answering service that morning, Pedro left the hotel, picked up a newspaper and went out for breakfast. But he never got to eat. As soon as he read the article on Wanda's death, he knew he needed to call Angela Porter right away. Why did they use his damn name? He hadn't wanted the public to know about his connection to Wanda and the Las Vegas murders. Until now, he had let Helena Swann run with that assumption about Porter and casino fraud. If she and Angela figured out by themselves that Porter was a murder suspect, Pedro would lose control of the situation.

He had to be the one to inform them that Samson Porter was the Las Vegas butcher—after he was paid.

His whole strategy to avoid legal trouble depended on it. Any complaint from them that they were bribing him to suppress that information would be an admission they were willing to obstruct justice. They'd never risk it. Pedro was just a guy with a client who wanted information. The money was merely a fee for that information. *As you can see, Counselor, Mr. Brunetti was duty bound to let Mrs. Porter know that her husband was under suspicion.*

He left the fried egg sandwich on the coffee shop counter with a five dollar bill. Out in the street, he pulled out his cell phone and dialed the number for the Marina District mansion. He could tell the call was being forwarded. A man's voice answered. This was not good.

"Pardon me," he said. "I may have the wrong number. Is Angela Porter there?"

"No, Angela isn't here. This is Brad Styles. And you must be Pedro Brunetti."

He knew he'd never see the money if he hung up now. He didn't.

"You'll have to excuse me, Mr. Styles, but Mrs. Swann said her sister wanted to do business with me. Would you have her call me, please?"

"I do have a package that I assume is for you, Mr. Brunetti. I'm not at all sure I'll give it to you. However, if you want to meet with me, I'm willing to talk the whole thing over. I'm concerned about the safety of Mrs. Swann and Mrs. Porter, so we'll have to do this right away, if at all."

So Brad Styles needed information. And Pedro certainly had some.

"Look, Mr. Styles, I think my research will be useful to you. However, information is worth something. Meet me in Union Square within ten minutes and bring the package with you. I'll be the fat man with dark hair in the tan suit, holding a soft hat."

"I'll be the guy with the manila envelope. And I'll be there in five minutes."

Styles was right on time. He was slim, above average height, thinning brown hair, pleasant looking, carried himself well. Pedro nodded when he saw him, and Styles sat down near him on the bench. There were plenty of people in the park as always—people walking through, people standing, people sitting on the benches. Pedro thought of Gene Hackman in *The Conversation*, bugging that couple in broad daylight. Right here in Union Square. It didn't do much for his confidence.

"What information do you have on Sam Porter, Mr. Brunetti?"

"Hasn't Helena Swann told you?" he said.

"Please don't stall. I want to know *now* what you have on Sam Porter."

"Are you prepared to give me that package?"

"Yes, Brunetti, but you don't really want it. If I give you the package, I'll tell the police everything. But I'm willing to give you a check for five thousand dollars just to get the full story. A legitimate transaction, Brunetti. Completely above board, no repercussions."

He thought of what it says in Jeremiah: *The harvest is past, the summer is ended, and we are not saved.* So was Pedro's harvest past, and he was able only to take the last gleanings of the field. Well, it was at least a sure thing.

"Write out the check and let me see it, Styles. And in the memo section, write down 'Report on S. Porter'."

From an inside jacket pocket, Brad Styles took out a checkbook and a gold Mont Blanc pen. When the check was filled out, he held it up so Pedro could see.

He nodded. "Sam Porter is suspected in the murder of two people in Las Vegas. The police will eventually look to match his DNA with a sample from the murder scene. He left Las Vegas the night of the murders and met your fiancée on his flight. You probably know that. You may not know whether she saw the murder scene, but I suspect she did. Finally, the police will sooner or later look at either Mickey Cullion or Porter for Wanda Buckley's murder. That I'm sure of."

It looked to Pedro like Brad's worst fears had been confirmed. He snatched at the check and got it. Styles just looked at his empty hand for a moment, then took off running—through the crowd, past a palm tree at the edge of the park, and out into the street.

CHAPTER 40

JOURNAL'S END

LIEUTENANT VIEJO

SHOO-FLY'S EMBEZZLEMENT SCHEME was a simple one, and pretty well thought out. Brad Styles had authorized him to request checks for himself or other Sharples employees for minor expenses. Brad didn't notice that these so-called minor charges could be as much as forty-five hundred dollars. The memo specifying the rules should have read *four hundred fifty dollars*. Shoo-fly slipped it by him, and Brad signed the memo to Cash Disbursements. It was still embezzlement, but the check issuance was covered. The whole thing would be clean on audit, unless they attempted to match the checks to goods and services received.

Shoo-fly had already cashed all the checks issued in his own name. He was supposed to give Mickey the checks made out to him when they split, until he decided to kill him. After he stole Mickey's wallet with ID, birth certificate and social security card, he set up a bank account and deposited those checks. He figured he'd be out of town before he'd be able to withdraw that money, but he was counting on getting it via bank draft before the fraud was detected at Sharples. All told, he would have fifty thousand dollars. The total for Mickey's checks would be twenty grand. Out of the thirty thousand that Shoo-fly would have clear for now, he'd put five thousand aside for Mickey—who would be expecting twenty. To make it look like more, it would be in fives and tens.

He got started early that last morning, completely energized after a night in the sack with Helena. At first, he devoted himself entirely to Angela, keeping her calm and centered through breakfast. Just holding her hand pointed up the difference between the gals. Angela's hand sat in his as a small, limp and compliant thing. Had it been Helena, she'd return pressure for pressure, prodding his palm with her nails to make her presence felt.

At six forty-five, Shoo-fly drove into the fog-laden city. Everywhere, lights winked through the mist in aid of the tardy sun. He thought of early morning in places like Arizona and Montana, so utterly different in mood and light. But *his* mood was high and fine—he had seldom felt better or more confident. Yes, he had hoped for more in the beginning, something permanent and stable, but that was already in the past. His future was *now*. He had always had a philosophy of high hopes— but low expectations. Count on a brighter day tomorrow, but if it crashes and burns, you need to shrug it off and go right on.

At the Prado hotel, he picked up his mail from the day before at the front desk and took the elevator to his room. Once inside, he opened the envelopes. The only new checks were in Mickey's name. They amounted to under a thousand dollars. He put them to one side for the moment.

From the room safe, he brought out his notebooks and two large envelopes with all the money from checks he had cashed earlier. The notebooks went in his briefcase, a leather lawyer's satchel. There was a group of eight one-thousand-dollar bills in one of the envelopes. Three he put in his wallet. Five he would bring to the bank and have changed into small denominations for the package Helena would give to Mickey. The balance of the money from already-cashed checks was in hundreds, fifties and twenties, all of which he stuffed into the satchel. Last, he made out a deposit ticket for the checks he had set aside earlier.

Finally, he packed the clothes he would take with him into his old suitcase. Just before leaving the hotel, he looked at himself in the mirror, checking to see that the shoulder holster with his forty-five wasn't visible against the smooth line of his suit jacket.

After he finished with the bank, Shoo-fly drove over to the street corner where he had promised to meet Helena and handed her the package for Mickey. When he arrived at Sharples Communications, he immediately bought a newspaper in the lobby and went to his office, where he read the story on Wanda's murder and decided time was running out fast.

He left messages for everyone with whom he had scheduled appointments, requesting postponements. Our call to interview him presented a challenge—should he handle it now, or postpone it and run? He had enough confidence in himself to think that he could satisfy us temporarily. That in itself could gain him hours, even a day.

As soon as I left Sharples Communications with Detectives Bowers and Bennett, Shoo-fly switched his office phone to voice mail, and told a member of his product team that he would be gone for a while, perhaps for the day. He left work with that big briefcase of his, which had been staring right at us while we interviewed him, propped up on his desk. The suitcase he had packed with clothes was already in his car. To lay a phony trail for himself, he stopped at the bus station, showed his ID and paid for a one-way ticket to Billings, Montana with his American Express card.

There was one more thing to do before leaving San Francisco. He would drive home and convince Helena to come away with him. If Angela was there, he'd just have to deal with that. She didn't matter. Where he would go depended entirely on Helena. Could he convince her to stick by him?

When he pulled up to the mansion gates, he paused to look at the fountain in the center of the cobblestone drive. Flowers and ivy surrounded the base while bright streams of water cascaded over the figures of satyrs and nymphs above. Both Helena's car and Angela's were in the driveway. He pulled in and parked behind them.

Shoo-fly had loved his life here. The mansion, the Porsche, Helena . . . but mostly the feeling of being somebody with money and power. Before going inside, he must have spent a few moments thinking and making notes in his journal . . . because this is where it ends.

CHAPTER 41

BOULDER IN THE ROAD

BY THE TIME HELENA LEFT MICKEY, found her car and drove home, Angela was already there. She must have finished with Brunetti, Helena thought. With both Mickey and the detective out of the way, maybe things could resume a normal course. Well, she supposed *normal* wasn't at all the right word. Still, if all that was behind them, she'd be able to think straight at last. As much as Helena wanted to hurl herself into her passion for Sam, a badgering voice reminded her about Brad Styles and her equally potent longing for the security wealth would bring. At the very least, she had been disabused of the notion that she could have both.

Esther had the day off after breakfast, so Angela would be alone. Helena walked into the foyer, looked for her in the library and called out her name. She heard a faint reply and judged it to have come from the terrace. Through the French doors, she saw her sister sitting quietly, hands in her lap. Angela was gazing out towards the bay, perched on the edge of her chair.

As Helena opened the doors, Angela turned to look up with a placid, yet searching gaze. An errant sea breeze sneaked in from the bay, cool and damp.

"Has Brad called you, Helena?" she asked.

"No, not today," she said, hugging herself against the sudden chill.

"Oh. I wonder if he called Sam?"

"Angela, why are you asking about Brad? Tell me how it went with Brunetti."

"I didn't see Brunetti. Brad has my cell phone. I called him when the bank manager insisted I have an escort."

"Brad will get the call? Brad will see Brunetti?"

"I was hoping he had by now and would have called you."

"Called *me*?"

"Yes, well, he hasn't called me, so I supposed . . . ."

"Why didn't you call Sam or me first, Angela? Why Brad?"

"I guess I didn't think of you as an escort. And Sam told me how busy he'd be today. He gets . . . upset when I call him at work."

"But Brad . . . Brad's the last person who would understand the situation."

Angela shook her head, confused.

"Why are we arguing about Brad, dear? What is it?"

Helena lost it then. Legally, Sam was her sister's husband. And from his long employment, Brad somehow belonged to her as well. For once, her bitter feelings about this spilled over.

"Maybe we're arguing about Brad because he's the only thing in the world that's mine alone. Maybe it's because you just call for him and take him whenever you want."

"Oh, Helena! I didn't mean . . . you know I couldn't . . . ."

She had hurt her deeply, and tears sprung from her sister's eyes.

"You know, Angela, you are so . . . insulated against the everyday world. Your money is like some wonderful buffer against anything sharp or nasty. I love you for the person you are, but your money makes you into some kind of untouchable—a plaster saint that I'd like to pull off its pedestal."

Helena had gone too far. Angela was silent for a moment, but her demeanor said that her eyes had opened, perhaps fully for the first time. She wiped her cheeks with the back of her hand and spoke in anger. "Money, money . . . always money. It's all you ever think of, isn't it? I think father left it all to me just so half of it, your half, wouldn't be spent on some incredible orgy of gambling, drugs and sex in Los Angeles or New York or . . . Las Vegas. Yes, that's it, Las Vegas, where everything started this time!"

"Look, I'm sorry. I shouldn't have said . . . ."

"That's right, you shouldn't have said anything at all. You talk about Brad and my presumptions when you know he's completely devoted to you. When you know how happy I've been to see some stability— finally—in one of your relationships."

"Angela, don't . . . ."

"Oh, if you only knew how often I've wondered about Sam and you and why you act so oddly with each other. First you meet in Las Vegas, then he calls on you here. Next you're totally apathetic to him while I dance with him and begin to fall in love."

"Please stop it!"

"Afterwards, the both of you so studiously keeping your distance in front of me. Bantering one moment, pulling faces at one another the next. And now, Helena, why have you gotten so completely involved in his problems? What does it all mean?"

Helena would have liked to cry. But it seemed this was a fight that could hurt her if she weren't careful. Instead of replying, she glared back and held her tongue. Unexpectedly, Angela bolted from the terrace and through the French doors into the house.

She knew she must follow and talk to Angela, but she waited a moment to quell the impulse to retaliate in kind, to slash and burn. As she walked off the terrace and into the living room, her cell phone rang. She plucked it out of her bag and answered.

It was Brad. He was speaking very quickly and

sounded anxious.

"Helena, is Angela there?"

"Yes, she is. Did you meet with Brunetti, Brad?"

"No questions, Helena, please. You have to get out of the house with Angela. The police are on their way, but get out of there now. Sam is no casino thief—he's a murderer. He killed those people you saw in Las Vegas, and he probably killed Wanda Buckley. He left work and may be headed home. Take Angela and go, Helena, right now! Call me as soon as you're out."

Sometimes the human mind doesn't process things quickly enough. Every word Brad uttered was clear and definitive, but it made no sense to Helena. And then she thought of Mickey, how scared and pale he was. She already knew by Sam's own admission he tried to murder the little man. And if he murdered those people in Las Vegas, yes, of course he would go on to kill poor Wanda. But she loved him, didn't she? How could that be, a murderer, the psycho kind who sliced women up like lunchmeat and cut men's balls off. She thought of Lana's little dog quivering in the corner of the kitchen, the terrible smells there and the pleading eyes of the corpses, open in abject horror.

Helena was standing stock still in the living room, half in shock and wondering where to turn, when the front door opened and Sam walked in like grim fate. Only he was smiling—smiling!

Because she hadn't ended the call from Brad, Helena dropped the cell phone into her open bag, praying he would hear whatever happened next. Sam might have caught the scent of her sudden fear, but he wouldn't have seen the cell phone from where he stood.

Hoping to cover any suspicion he had, Helena pretended to look for something.

"Something wrong?" he asked. "I don't have much time, Helena. The cops . . . ."

"Sam, Wanda Buckley's been murdered."

He nodded. "I saw the newspaper. We'll talk about it later. Right now I want you to leave town with me."

Trance-like, she walked up to him in the foyer.

"Did Angela ever tell you I saw those bodies in Wanda's house?"

"She did, yes. But I thought you saw just one body."

"No, I saw them both."

"And you never panicked. You stayed cool."

He said it admiringly. They stood close now. She could see the beads of perspiration on his forehead. She could smell him.

"Were you the one, Sam, did you do those terrible things?"

His whole face contracted somehow, the color rising to his cheeks. His nostrils flared out, and his lips tightened into a bitter line. A slow smile revealed the white teeth and the deep dimples. When he spoke, his voice was laced with sarcasm.

"Figured it all out, have we? Or maybe you've been talking to somebody."

"Oh, Sam, I'm so tired. This has been hard on me, the business with Mickey, then Brunetti. I'll go with you, Sam, but you have to let me speak to Angela first. I can't go without letting her know."

He seemed to relax a little, believing in her now, thinking she would leave with him.

"Look Helena, I don't want to see Angela if I can help it. Just tell her you're going out and she shouldn't worry. She probably hasn't seen my car or she'd already be down here. But do it quick, Helena, there's no time."

She raced out of the living room and glanced into the library, where she almost missed her. Angela was sitting in one of the two club chairs that faced the fireplace and had their high backs to the doorway. Helena happened to see a foot move, and walked in. As she spoke to the back of the chair, her whisper came out distorted and trembling to her own ears.

"Angela, Brad just called. He met with Brunetti. It was Sam murdered Wanda Buckley and those people in Las Vegas. He's a killer, Angela. He's demented and cruel."

Angela rose from her chair and turned to face her. Her bearing was steady and regal, but there was cold anger in her face.

"Helena, stop it! How can you do this? Sam's no murderer, that's absurd. What are you trying to do to us?"

"Please, Angela, you know things aren't right. You even said so. This is what has been wrong all along."

She just wanted to get Angela and herself into one of the upstairs rooms where they could lock the door and stall for time, or even signal to someone from a window. But you never know how other people will think or react. Angela was not to be swept away. She was duty and devotion, a boulder in the road stopping all traffic.

"If Sam's in trouble, he needs me. He'll want money, and . . . ."

"Angela, please! Leave him to the police. They'll be here soon."

"No, he's my husband, of course I'll help him!"

Just then Sam walked in on them with an angry, crooked smile and sparkling eyes, holding by its strap with one forefinger the purse she must have dropped in the foyer as she turned to go. Her cell phone was in his other hand. He had shut it down.

"Thank you, Angela," he said. "Your devotion touches me, it really does. See, Helena, someone wants to help me."

"Sam, you have to go, darling," Angela said. "The police are coming to arrest you."

"Ah . . . . Helena's handiwork, no doubt."

She recoiled, pleading. "No Sam, you can't think I would have . . . ."

He shrugged, sneering. "Well, I do, Helena. And here I was thinking we're all family."

As he reached into his jacket, Angela took hold of his arm. Helena turned and ran from the room. When she heard the gunshot, she couldn't tell whether it was meant for her or whether he had shot Angela. *Oh no, not that,* she thought. *That would surely damn me to hell!*

Fleeing upstairs, she had just reached her room when she heard a high-decibel cracking noise in the foyer. Loud voices and scuffling sounds followed. The front door had been splintered by a battering ram, and policemen were invading the mansion.

For the first time in her life, Helena became hysterical—screaming, crying, laughing. A few endless minutes went by before she understood that she and Angela were safe. When the detectives trudged up to her bedroom, she was unable to speak. Later, a doctor came to administer a sedative, and she found herself wishing it was an overdose.

Angela, on the other hand, had remained calm. She absolutely refused to cooperate with the police team or the detectives who followed. She claimed Sam hadn't been there. Since his Porsche was in the driveway and still warm, they thought she was hiding him. It took them precious minutes to perform a thorough search of the house.

So Sam got away, thanks to Angela. But his briefcase was there in the Porsche. When the black detective, Bowers, asked where the money came from, neither Helena nor Angela could say. But Brad knew—it was the only time he smiled all day.

The next morning, Helena learned that Sam fled

through the back entrance and onto a neighbor's property.

"What did he say, Angela?" she asked.

"Nothing I want to repeat. He had this look in his eyes . . . I need to forget that. Thinking he'd need money, I fumbled into my bag and handed him my wallet. He snatched it and vaulted out the door. Then he disappeared through a hedge."

Later, the Costanzas next door reported one of their cars stolen.

Brad stayed with Helena and Angela that awful first night, checking on them from time to time and getting workers over to board up the entrance. It was he who requested the doctor to come and sedate Helena. Other than asking if she were all right, he didn't make conversation with her. His manner was cool, and she knew she had lost him. Was it for good?

CHAPTER 42

THE WHOLE SCREWED UP STORY

WHEN MICKEY CULLION TOLD Helena to get the fuck out of his car, he took off thinking he'd leave town right away and never again in his whole life see San Francisco or anybody connected with Sam Porter. Looking down at that envelope, though, he realized he'd have to stop somewhere and count the money before moving on. It was pretty fat, but you can never tell. Where he could lay low had a lot to do with how well-fixed he was. To complicate matters, he had no ID and no way of getting one without risking cop trouble. Besides, he was a genuine meltdown mess after living two days in his car. He still felt shitty from the blood loss, and forty-eight hours with no shower had left him ripe and cranky.

He decided to risk going back to his apartment. Sam would be out of town for sure—with or without Helena, so he wasn't afraid of the big man anymore. And the cops would only be looking for him when they suspected it was his blood and puke in Wanda's room. He didn't intend to stay long, just count the money and get cleaned up. That would be an hour tops. He wanted to be out of San Francisco before noon.

He parked on the same side street, about a block away from his building, then walked back, envelope in hand. When he started into the lobby, Pedro Brunetti was suddenly right behind him. Fatso was getting better at a tail.

"Mickey Cullion, I presume. I was just coming over to toss your crib. But this is so much nicer."

This apparently was his way of talking cool. Mickey

had the point of his knife in Pedro's face before he could react.

"Go ahead and move you fat fuck, and you'll look like Jack Nicholson in that movie where the little pervert slits his nose open."

Pedro put his hands up quick.

"Mickey, I never pack. You can check. Go ahead."

Mickey searched him, giving his balls a good rake when he went into his crotch, just for the hell of it. Pedro stiffened, but he took it.

"Okay, will you put the knife away now?"

"Depends. First, let's hear what you're after."

"The thing you need to hear most is that the police are surely looking for Sam Porter right now. Brad Styles knows he's a murderer, so I would think Porter no longer has a home to go to."

"Like I would care."

"Oh, I think you do. Be that as it may, I'm here for my own mercenary reasons. I lost a client on this deal because of the rash Mr. Porter. I also lost the chance to extract good money from the Sharples empire."

"Brunetti, you're boring me to death here."

"And you, my friend, look like death warmed over. Lose some blood, did we?"

"The story worth something to you?"

"The story of you and your friend may be worth something to a sharp reporter I know. I couldn't get much money out of Brad Styles, and now all that's left is the cash value of an eyewitness account. Which is where you come in. Please put that knife down!"

Mickey flipped it closed but held it ready in his palm. He was sure now Shoo-fly *hadn't* turned Brunetti. That was just bullshit Helena tried to feed him. He motioned Pedro toward the stairs. The fat man wheezed up the two flights with Mickey behind not doing much better.

When they reached the apartment, Mickey flopped on the ratty purple couch, and Pedro took a kitchen chair.

"Tell you what, Brunetti, I'm going to the head and get cleaned up. If you're still here when I'm done, I'll give you your story for a certain . . . consideration."

"And what would that be?"

"I need a fake ID, a good one, and the means to get it. What connections do you have?"

A wide smile spread over Pedro's big moon face.

"Go to the bathroom and perform your ablutions, my boy. Those kinds of connections I have. When you're ready, we'll leave directly from here and get you that ID—my treat."

By one o'clock Mickey was on the road with a new identity. Silas Esteban—could he even remember it? They bought a good-looking state of California ID with his new moniker not two blocks away in the Mission district. That Brunetti was good for something after all, besides spouting bible verses. Mickey had planned on lifting his wallet, but didn't have the heart after he came through for him.

When he counted the money in the envelope from Sam, there was only five grand. The bastard cheated him by at least fifteen. He related the whole screwed up story of him and Shoo-fly Porter and Helena Swann, leaving out certain details that would tend to incriminate him. It was a helluva tale. Good thing Pedro had one of those little digital recorders. He said Mickey should look for the story in the newspapers. He would keep his own name out of it, the whole thing would look like an interview with Mickey and this reporter guy.

Well, sure, why not? He didn't give a crap now. Mickey Cullion? Never heard of him. His name was . . . Silas Esteban.

CHAPTER 43

MADE FOR MURDER

LIEUTENANT VIEJO

RIGHT AFTER SHOO-FLY GOT AWAY from us in the Marina district, I became part of a task force in San Francisco, on loan from Las Vegas. Bowers and I took the notebooks in Shoo-fly's briefcase and classified them as confidential in both the San Francisco and Las Vegas investigations. I took custody of the notebook leading up to and including the murders at Wanda Buckley's house. Bowers appropriated the notebook Shoo-fly started in San Francisco.

We each photocopied our documents and exchanged them, so that each of us had a complete set— the original pertaining to the crimes in his own jurisdiction, and the photocopy pertaining to the other's case. Taken as a whole, we referred to these notebooks as 'the journal.' The journal would be some of our best evidence if we could ever bring this prick to justice.

The first lead after his escape was finding the Costanzas' stolen Lexus in the Castro, the district of San Francisco famous for the high percentage of gay men living there. From this came a new headline and a spurious story. The headline said:

PSYCHO BI LOVER CRUISED CASTRO

The story went on to document a number of sightings of a man fitting Shoo-fly's description cruising bars and taking other men back to an apartment where he mistreated them in various ways. None of the leads went anywhere. Inflamed imaginations were seeing

Sam Porter as they might have spotted Elvis at the local Seven Eleven. Every butch, dark-haired gay man in San Francisco was being reported to us on the hotline. And brother, there are plenty of them.

The Lexus didn't yield evidence of any real significance, just a few fast food wrappers that indicated he consumed a couple of meals there before abandoning it. After a week of fruitless searches in the Castro, each one of them causing a new complaint of police harassment, we shifted our focus to notifying police departments in the western tier of states. Bowers and I knew that Shoo-fly's purchase of a bus ticket to Montana was a red herring. But the brass played it up big, and the press followed hungrily. So more resources were expended in vain. What's new, right?

I was dropped from the task force soon after we abandoned the search in San Francisco. Bowers and Bennett and I promised to stay in touch on any new developments. All of us wondered and speculated where Shoo-fly was hiding. Back home at last, I took a few days vacation time. The wife hadn't seen me in weeks, so the usual yard work and household chores had gotten hopelessly behind. I puttered around and enjoyed my Ellen's company for three days plus the weekend. I took her out to eat every night and even went shopping with her once. Which I was happy to do for a change.

On the Friday, though, I noticed an article in the paper about a bar brawl in Reno. Now that sent a chill down my spine. As I read it, I thought about Shoo-fly's jail term and what he said about bringing his boxing prowess into the bars. Sure enough, the guy's description checked out—big guy, well-dressed, dark hair.

It seems some cowboy made a remark everybody thought was pretty innocent. Except the big guy, that is, who got up off his stool and started throwing punches. The cowboy was no slouch either, getting in a left jab or two before our hero broke his nose, and the guy went down. Right after the altercation, the big fellow took off in an old, beat up Taurus. The Reno police were still looking for him.

I hesitated before calling Reno, because I didn't want some reporter getting wind of my name and drawing a conclusion that would lead to more publicity. In my mind, the thing was this—if Shoo-fly went from San Francisco to Reno, what would be his next destination? Las Vegas? Could be. So I briefed the chief and asked a junior colleague to make some discreet calls to the authorities in Reno. I'd have him take a ride up there if they found that Taurus. Shoo-fly might have ditched it and left evidence behind. Then I tried to forget about the whole thing for the weekend.

~ ~ ~

Rupert McAllister, a pushy investigative journalist for the San Francisco Chronicle, first came onto the scene around that time. He called us to corroborate certain aspects of the case that hadn't been made public. When I asked Maynard Bennett about him, he verified his credentials and told me McAllister had been in touch with him as well.

Let me tell you, the media can make an investigation impossible. They'll rip you a new one for not having a suspect. Then they'll excoriate you for naming a suspect if your case isn't ironclad. They dog our steps, get in our way, and blow leads by publishing them rather than letting us follow up. You can't win with them, and after a while you don't try.

I saw some asshole just last night on TV pontificating about the proper relationship of the press to the government being one of "skeptical opposition." Maybe it's just me, but skeptical opposition assumes everything the government does is suspect, and guarantees conflict and unfairness. Which is what cops get every day from those bastards.

And yet, every detective sooner or later finds that he needs the press to help get information out. So I have to admit there are good reporters out there who listen and try to do the right thing. I've worked with them any number of times. I just wish there were more.

McAllister's first big story on Shoo-fly was so sensational that we had a burgeoning media frenzy on our hands. Instead of changing from a regional to a national story, it went international. British, French, German, Italian, Japanese, and Dutch reporters were making inquiries within the first week.

This tall, pasty-faced individual with his greasy hair and British accent somehow engineered an interview with Mickey Cullion before he fled the scene. Mickey wasn't wanted for a crime at that moment, so McAllister hadn't done anything wrong, but how the hell did he know about him, and how was he the first to find him? There was certainly a leak somewhere, but we didn't find it.

This was McAllister's story:

SHOO-FLY PORTER:
SOCIALITE PSYCHO
IN THE EXECUTIVE SUITE

by Rupert McAllister

The images are indelible. First, the blood-spattered rooms with mutilated corpses in two cities. Then, the Marina district mansion replete with fountains and gardens where Shoo-fly chased and shot at his socialite lover in front of her terrified sister—who happens to be his devoted wife.

But it all started back on the Las Vegas
Strip where Shoo-fly plied his daytime
trade as casino dealer and played his
nighttime role as deadly lover of both
women and men.

How can we quantify evil? A good start
would be to catch its most degenerate
proponent and calculate the horrors in his
psyche. Catching Sam "Shoo-fly" Porter,
however, has proved problematic for two
big-city police departments. He first eluded
capture in Las Vegas. And now he has
evaded our San Francisco lawmen and
remains at large: armed and extremely
dangerous. Be afraid, America. Be very
afraid.

It was Michael Lester Cullion who gave
us this story. Everyone knows him as
Mickey, a little guy who was Shoo-fly's
friend and lover for five years. Until Shoo-
fly turned on him and cut his throat, that is.
Mickey nearly bled to death on the very
same day Wanda Buckley was butchered in
her San Francisco hotel room.

Wanda was a rich Las Vegas real estate
agent looking into the murder of a friend. A
source close to the investigation says Shoo-
fly jammed a broken whisky bottle into her
throat so viciously that she was nearly
decapitated. Who can this maniac be? What
kind of life produces such a monster?

And as if these heinous crimes weren't
enough, sources in Las Vegas claim that
Shoo-fly had previously gutted two victims
at Wanda Buckley's house in a fashionable
suburb there. Lana Firewood was Wanda's

best friend, a party girl and sometime mistress of Shoo-fly who had her neck snapped and her breasts and other organs mutilated with a cleaver. Randy Prinz was cleavered as well, at the same grisly scene, with the exception that his testicles were chopped off and stuffed into his mouth. Was this Shoo-fly's warning to any man bold enough to cut in on his action?

We asked Mickey where he met Shoo-fly Porter. "In prison," he said. "I'm just a little guy and I needed protection. Shoo-fly gave me that in return for the usual favors."

What was Porter's background?

"His mother was a prostitute in Chicago. He hated that and left home in his teens," Cullion said. "He was a prizefighter in Tucson, a bartender, bouncer, ranch hand in Montana and a casino dealer in Vegas. He got a college degree in prison and had a job with Blue Cross in Arizona for a while."

But it's Shoo-fly's transition from casino dealer in Las Vegas to high-powered business executive for Sharples Communications in San Francisco that boggles the mind.

"You gotta understand that Shoo-fly was real smart and real ambitious," says Cullion. "But his temper usually brings him down. He don't think right when he gets mad."

The most astonishing aspect of the case is Porter's association with one of San Francisco's most illustrious families: the Sharples. Angela Sharples married Samson

Porter in the "Society Wedding of the Year"
just a few weeks ago after a whirlwind
romance. But Shoo-fly wasn't satisfied with
just one of the Sharples sisters. He needed
both of them, according to Mickey Cullion.

"Helena Swann is the stepsister, I
think," said Cullion. "She's very pretty, but a
real snob who wouldn't give you the time of
day. Shoo-fly was crazy about her."

Now the Sharples family have refused
to give this reporter a statement of any
kind, but we note that Michael Lester
Cullion was a guest at the wedding of
Angela Sharples to Samson Porter. And
Cullion says Helena Sharples Swann was
definitely Samson Porter's Delilah.
Sometimes, he called her Helena Troia, an
obvious wordplay on Helen of Troy.

This story has only just begun. The
police have released few details of their
investigation. We understand a nationwide
manhunt may be announced soon. Other
sources have told us that a detective from
the Las Vegas Police Department is aiding
the investigation.

And the nickname "Shoo-fly," where did
that come from?

"Well," says Cullion, "he don't like to be
called that no more. But he told me when he
was a little kid his mother used to buy shoo-
fly pies at a nearby bakery. So every time
she comes home from shopping, he yells:
Shoo-fly! Shoo-fly! His mother thinks its
funny and starts calling him Shoo-fly. So it
stuck. He told me he used to douse them
with ketchup and gobble them up."

If there was such a thing as an intergalactic story, this would have been it. Like a snowball rolling downhill into hell, it accumulated everything in its path until it became gargantuan and noxious, and finally rolled hissing into the cauldron, passing into legend. Truly, it was stupefying.

Somehow that business about how he got the nickname made me think Sam Porter was doomed from childhood. I think what he liked about those shoo-fly pies as a kid was the way they looked when he mashed them up and added ketchup. Like the blood and gore of his future victims.

If ever a man was made for murder, it was Shoo-fly.

CHAPTER 44

SOME THINGS NEVER CHANGE

THE ODIOUS NARRATIVE in the Chronicle by Rupert McAllister destroyed Helena Swann's reputation in San Francisco. The deluge of sympathy that came her way after being abused and shot at evaporated overnight. People stared at her and whispered. Friends stopped calling. Neither Angela nor Brad gave any credence to Mickey Cullion's scurrilous remarks, calling the whole thing tabloid journalism at its lowest. And Helena believed Angela was sincere in this, but Brad . . . well, Brad was just trying not to pile on after having dumped her for the awful liability she had become.

At least Cullion hadn't said anything about the money she delivered to him on behalf of Sam. Somehow Helena thought that was his way of letting her off the hook. Because of that omission, the police still had no reason to suspect her of involvement in any crime. The affair everyone was sure she had with Sam wasn't police business, and Angela was good enough to dismiss even those allegations out of hand.

That was wishful thinking, of course, and whether or not Angela had reservations, Helena was grateful for the favor. To give herself due credit, she would have admitted everything to her sister. Even the sordid details. She owed Angela the truth, if asked, and would have taken the consequences. But Angela was Angela— she did not ask.

Brad had engaged a security detail to guard the mansion. Nonetheless, Helena was anxious about Sam returning to kill her. After all, she was Delilah now, his downfall, the seductress who sheared his locks—and the whole world knew how vindictive he was at any betrayal.

So she left town quietly, shortly after giving her deposition to the police. Only Angela knew at first, telling Brad when she had gone. A month or two in Newport would help her avoid the publicity she seemed to attract everywhere she went in California. Here was a chance to renew her warm ties to Ivan Chitworth and her Aunt Claudia. Ivan, in fact, was the only relative or friend who could actually make her smile about her newfound notoriety.

San Francisco had become a prison where bad memories and self-doubt dogged Helena. There were constant reminders there of her venality and her shame. A change of scene would quiet her fears about Sam and ease her frazzled sensibilities. Best of all, Ivan and she could laugh at the whole evil world, including themselves, just as they had when they were children.

Arriving in Boston on Saturday afternoon, she checked into the Westin at Copley Square for the weekend. Ivan picked her up on Monday for the hour and a half drive to Newport. As they sailed over the bridges in Narragansett Bay, first to Jamestown, then Newport, she grew enchanted with the sparkling harbor scenes of sun and sky, sailboats and period architecture. Ivan chattered away while Helena was lost in a world of cherished childhood memory.

The final mile down Bellevue Avenue astonished her. It was still exactly the same. Ivan noticed her tears as they flew past the Reading Room, the Redwood Library, the Art Museum and the wonderful old commercial block with the Newport Casino. Soon they had passed De La Salle and the Elms and were at Leroy Avenue, where they turned left for Dismas Cottage. It felt more like home than anything she had known for years.

"Okay, babe. Here we are. Dry those tears before mother sees them and thinks I violated you or something."

"Oh, Ivan, doesn't she know about you yet?" I laughed.

"Hope springs eternal, Helena. Some things never change."

"Like Newport, I guess."

She spent hours alone on the garden paths of Dismas Cottage that first week. The grounds had been designed by Frederick Law Olmstead and were counted as one of Newport's historical treasures. Aunt Claudia opened them to the public on the first Saturday of each month from August through October.

Occasionally, refreshments were served as she and Ivan sat under one of the enormous weeping beeches towards the back of the property. So cool was it under those trees on even the warmest day that her aunt ordered hot tea. Claudia's little rituals were so practiced and ancient by now that Helena would never dream of making a request for some iced alternative. That would break the sweet spell and propel them back into the brutal present—the world of Shoo-fly stories and television reality shows. Who needed that? And that hideous nickname for Sam that everyone used now? She couldn't bear to hear it.

What a dear Aunt Claudia was. To her, Helena was still that little girl of twenty and more summers ago, running barefoot through the house and begging her stepfather to take her to the beach. Did she ever wonder about the awful stories in the magazines and newspapers? Somehow Helena hoped not. At any rate, Claudia and Ivan were helping to keep her presence in Newport a secret.

For his part, Ivan was lovely company except, of course, for the nights he went out with friends. He would ask her to come along, but she wasn't about to run with a herd of gay men. The epithet "fag hag" would have been a fatal last blow to her reputation and self-esteem.

All in all, Helena settled in at Dismas Cottage like a native Newporter—staying on the island, shopping locally, eating out occasionally, sunbathing at Bailey's Beach, and poring over old books at the Redwood Library. After a time, Las Vegas and San Francisco and the things that happened there were reduced to a kind of chronic disease one is forced to live with. She could manage the pain, even though a cure was out of the question.

CHAPTER 45

WHITED SEPULCHRES

PEDRO BRUNETTI LEFT San Francisco free of legal complications. The money from Brad Styles wasn't so much, and the payment from McAllister for Mickey's story was even less—but all in all it made up for the loss of his client. Poor Wanda, of course, had lost everything. Still, Pedro retained an interest in the case, and he followed it like everybody else in America when he got back to Las Vegas. With his buddy Janeway of the LVPD still part of the investigation, he was able to follow it even closer.

The whole world knew that Sam Porter escaped from San Francisco, but almost nobody knew that Helena Swann had left town. He learned that from Janeway—who got it in confidence from Viejo. With Mickey Cullion also in the wind, Pedro's thoughts ran to Matthew 3:7, *'Oh generation of vipers, who hath warned you to flee from the wrath to come?'* Which was no joke to him—not in the least. Pedro was convinced that a generation of vipers was indeed loose in the world, and he often wondered how God's wrath would manifest itself.

Janeway also told him about going to Reno to check out the old Taurus the guy in the bar brawl abandoned. The car was concealed in a shed outside town. And it might have remained there for a long time if the fellow who owned the property hadn't happened to come in from San Diego, where he lived. Nobody in Reno was supposed to find out about the connection to Shoo-fly, but Janeway let it slip, and the town's officialdom went crazy, from mayor to dogcatcher. Viejo barely managed to save him from being busted to patrolman.

Shoo-fly, of course, was long gone from Reno. The cops didn't pick up his trail again until he reached Phoenix. Shoo-fly—everybody was calling him that now, thanks to Rupert McAllister. What a media wizard that Englishman was—his newspaper story had Pedro holding his breath like he was hearing it for the first time. Thank God he was kept out of it, though. As a consequence, he hung on to his P.I. license.

McAllister got in touch with Pedro afterwards for a detailed conversation about his involvement in the Las Vegas and San Francisco investigations. As soon as the police caught Porter, he planned to write what he hoped would be the definitive book on the affair. While he wanted to give Pedro credit for the Mickey Cullion interview, among other things, Pedro backed away— refusing to leave himself open to litigation. In the end, McAllister agreed to name him only in those well-documented parts of the story that wouldn't make for legal complications.

Pedro's real contribution to McAllister's book came when he quoted Matthew to sum up the leading miscreants, Shoo-fly and Helena—*Ye are like unto whited sepulchres, which indeed appear beautiful outward, but are within full of dead men's bones, and of all uncleanness.*

McAllister nearly creamed his jeans over that. No doubt he thought a spicy bible verse would add juice to the drama. That wasn't Pedro's intent, however. He thought of himself and McAllister as full of that same corruption—the stink of the grave given off by the unregenerate.

CHAPTER 46

A BANK IN PHOENIX

LIEUTENANT VIEJO

THE TOPLINE REASON WE DIDN'T want the media to hang the Shoo-fly tag on the Reno incident was the panic it would set off in Las Vegas. You could draw the conclusion he was working his way over to us again. The casino and hotel bigwigs, the Chamber of Commerce and the mayor didn't want our precious tourists scared off. I didn't think Shoo-fly would be careless enough to come our way, but if he did, we were ready. All leaves were canceled indefinitely on the LV force and we were on "heightened alert," I guess you'd call it.

What finally brought the Reno story out in the open was Shoo-fly's visit to Phoenix several days later. The incident there started out as a local newspaper story, then blossomed into "Shoo-fly South," the third leg of the whole sorry mess. Just before that, we had this period of respite during which the major newspapers had moved the story off page one, even though the tabloids and the scandal rags kept the thing alive with clever headlines like:

ANGELS & DEMONS: ANGELA & BRAD VS. SHOO-FLY & HELENA

Anyway, here's the initial story from the Phoenix Sun before guys like Rupert McAllister jazzed it up:

UPROAR IN BANK BRANCH

by Larry Fender

The downtown branch of Phoenix Federal Savings Bank was the scene of a wild dustup yesterday afternoon when a customer erupted into violence while waiting for service. Freda Spence, a spokesperson for the bank, said that a customer whom she refused to identify was apparently upset by a delay in processing a draft on a San Francisco bank.

The man, described earlier by Benson Arroyo, branch manager, as a white male, dark-haired and tall, became enraged shortly after Mr. Arroyo left him to check on the status of the San Francisco bank account.

"He basically trashed my office," said Mr. Arroyo.

Bank employees and patrons watched in horror as the man overturned Mr. Arroyo's desk, spilling its contents onto the floor. Screaming obscenities, he withdrew a pistol from his suit jacket and fired a shot into the ceiling, setting off the sprinkler system.

"What bothers me most," said Mr. Arroyo, "was that he seemed to take great satisfaction in targeting the family picture I keep on my desk. After smashing it repeatedly against the overturned desk, he unzipped his trousers and urinated on it in full view of everybody."

The picture of Mr. and Mrs. Arroyo, their two children Amy and Gregg, and the family dog Pepper, was ruined. The bank, according to Ms. Spence, will not release the man's name or the exact nature and

> *status of the transaction in question, in order to insure customer privacy.*

If you haven't guessed, Shoo-fly was desperately trying to withdraw from the account he set up in Mickey Cullion's name back in San Francisco. He still looked respectable, but he was on the edge—in need of a shave, clothes somewhat rumpled. Not at all like the well-groomed fellow we remember. Almost certainly, he realized this was his last chance to get a little of his hard-earned dough. But it failed.

As a result of the reports he requested the day Shoo-fly fled, Brad Styles was able to help the San Francisco police establish the grounds for fraud almost immediately. All banks had been alerted to put a hold on any account in the name of Samson Porter or Michael Lester Cullion.

Still, Shoo-fly had enough money to keep himself going. We didn't know anything about Angela's wallet at the time, which contained over a thousand dollars in cash. Not a fortune by any means, but it was a secret she kept from us until much later.

CHAPTER 47

SO MUCH FOR GOOD INTENTIONS

LATELY, BRAD STYLES FOUND himself wondering why secrets had become so offensive to people in this country. He knew it wasn't always so. When he was younger, for instance, there were family secrets, secret handshakes, secrets you kept for best friends, government secrets—all kinds of information you might be privy to that you wouldn't think of revealing.

Today, if a guy knows something other people don't, he figures there must be a way to exploit it—elicit money or fame from it. It is all grist for the mill, fodder for the cannon, grease for the palm. The only one Brad knew anymore who could *really* keep a secret was Angela Sharples Porter. She wouldn't discuss Sam Porter with anyone, not even the police.

Certainly she never discussed him with Brad, until the day came she felt it necessary to issue a public statement. There were so many rumors about what she would or wouldn't do next, and there were so many inquiries from friends and relatives as well as the press—that she sought him out to craft a statement that would end the speculation.

One Sunday morning they sat on her terrace eating little pastries and drinking coffee from china cups while he jotted down her thoughts on what the statement should say. Brad produced a first draft, which Angela approved after making a couple of minor changes. Then he prevailed on her to submit it to her lawyer and one person—just one—from the Sharples public relations team. The result of this collaboration was a short press release stating Angela's position on the charges pending against Sam:

Angela Porter wishes to inform all those who have inquired that she plans to remain in San Francisco and will participate fully in the legal defense of her husband Sam Porter against the charges filed by the district attorney. Upon the return of Mr. Porter, she will support him in any and all efforts to clear himself. Mrs. Porter will issue no further statements regarding the charges against Mr. Porter or her future plans.

At the time, Brad thought this was pretty innocuous. And he agreed with Angela that it made sense to publish a definitive statement to stop the rumors about divorce and her possible testimony against Sam at trial. What they didn't count on was the dramatic simplicity of the statement striking a spark in the public imagination. Overnight, Angela became the steadfast heroine who would not fail the man she loved, not even in the face of public obloquy.

Instead of a page nine story in the California newspapers, Angela was front-page news everywhere. So much for good intentions.

~ ~ ~

About a month after Sam Porter fled from San Francisco, Brad was in his office at the Tremont building chatting with Angela about a charity dinner for Alzheimer's research. This was one of the few events she hosted every year, and he expected she would bow out this time. Which she did. But something else was on her mind as well.

"Brad, I need to see a doctor, but I don't want the paparazzi and tabloid vultures to find out. Help me, will you."

"Consider it done. Jack Gentile's your doctor, isn't he? I guarantee he'll make a house call for you. Want me to call him?"

"No, no. I could make a phone call. The problem is I

need an obstetrician to examine me. I've never had an obstetrician."

Brad dropped his eyes and felt his face go red. For a moment, he couldn't even look at her.

Angela laughed. "I see you understand," she said.

"Anything I say now is going to be wrong, Angela. If I say 'That's awful,' it's wrong. If I say ' Congratulations,' it's wrong."

She nodded. "I know. Just help me find a good doctor who will take me in after hours or something."

"Sure. We'll get you in under a different name. If somebody on his staff has to be there . . . maybe you could wear a wig."

She laughed again. "How about a bag over my head?"

"I'm glad you have a sense of humor about this, kid. I'm freaked out."

"I'm not . . . now. Maybe at first I was. Now I'm just trying to figure out how to get away at the right time, before I'm showing. Then again, maybe it's a false alarm."

It wasn't, of course. Angela was pregnant all right, with Sam Porter's child. She planned to stay in San Francisco right now, but would leave for the condo on Kauai in a few weeks. Brad was uneasy about her intention to hire a midwife and keep an obstetrician in reserve, but what could he say? She wanted to avoid a stay in a public hospital, and he wasn't about to argue with her.

He arranged the examination she wanted with Paul Clements, an obstetrician from Chicago who came to San Francisco at Brad's request. But the eminent doctor had a wife who couldn't hold her tongue. In 'strictest confidence,' she unburdened herself to an acquaintance who sold the information to Rupert McAllister. The story he filed on Angela's pregnancy was garnished with a repellent headline.

SON OF SAM RUMOR RAGES: SHOO-FLY'S ANGEL PREGNANT

The media exploded, and Brad felt the terrible power of the public's voyeurism. This level of intrusiveness was monstrous to him, criminal even. To keep Angela out of the crush, he opened his vacation home on Catalina for her, inviting her to stay until she was ready for Hawaii.

In the end, Angela took it philosophically, but Brad counted it as a personal failure. Before this, he couldn't fathom why well-known people punch out cameramen and reporters who harass them. It was crystal clear why now, and he longed to join their ranks. For a very private guy who disliked publicity, he was being put to the test. Even his domestic relations suffered. Whenever he visited his mother, she looked at him with that expression all mothers use to tell us what a disappointment we are to them. Her advice was to leave Sharples Communications and live on his trust fund. She gave no credence to the notion that a fellow might need a career to feel like a useful citizen.

Years before, his mother hadn't expressly disapproved when Brad began dating Helena in college, but he knew how she felt about the Sharples sisters. To Nuala Styles, Angela was a social equal, while Helena was practically an interloper. Adopted, rebellious and unpredictable—it was a description that didn't recommend itself to his mother. Nevertheless, Helena was a lot like her stepdad, much more so than his natural child. Sam Sharples had been a rebel, unpredictable and energetic—and ruthless when he had to be. Like so many men who launch successful businesses, he was a contrarian. Brad's attraction to Helena was on many levels, just like his admiration for her dad.

Although their first try at romance hadn't lasted, Brad and Helena became lovers after she separated from Jeremy Swann and moved back into Angela's home in the Marina District. Helena had never been far from his mind over the years, and the renewal of his passion seemed preordained. Now, their marriage plans were a shambles. Unlike Angela, who refused to face it or even consider it, Brad was convinced Helena had an affair with Sam Porter. That old yen for excitement reeled her in. You might say Brad should have seen it coming. And he did, but you can't untwist a tornado, you can only watch it level the landscape.

Before leaving San Francisco, Helena called Brad at work. She didn't tell him of her plans to go east, she only wanted to apologize.

"No excuses, Brad. I've made an awful mess. I wouldn't blame you for hating me."

He remained silent, afraid of what he might say if he got started.

"I can't even bring myself to ask your forgiveness," she said. "I only hope you'll find someone who'll treat you as you deserve."

She made no mention of trying again, for which he was thankful. Was it a performance? With Helena, how could you tell? Despite his silence and his coolness towards her, Brad thought of her every day. Would he ever move on?

CHAPTER 48

THE MEXICO THEORY

LIEUTENANT VIEJO

WHENEVER I CALLED Bowers or Bennett in San Francisco, I would try to interest them in tracking down Mickey Cullion. But it was no use. No bang for the buck, they said. They agreed he was an accomplice, and they read McAllister's stories like everybody else. But Cullion didn't tell *where* he got his throat cut, and you just knew he wasn't about to say he was in Wanda Buckley's room the night she was murdered. So that 'unidentified blood and vomitus' remained officially unidentified.

Naturally, they tossed his apartment, but there was nothing—he had stripped the bed of bedclothes, and there was no toothbrush or comb to use for DNA testing. We looked for relatives in Idaho, where he was born, without finding any.

I had an idea he would have gone to Mexico. It was the bellboy who said something, the kid who originally fell under suspicion for Wanda Buckley's murder. After McAllister's story broke, this kid got back to us about Mickey. Earlier, he couldn't recall anyone by the name of Sam Porter or Michael Cullion. The guy he knew as Mick didn't occur to him until he read McAllister's story and figured it had to be Cullion. I probed the kid for a good hour and found out that the places Mickey seemed nostalgic for were in Idaho and Mexico. He talked a lot about a trip he took to Baja once. There was no way I could follow up on my own because Mickey wasn't a suspect at all in Las Vegas.

Then I got the bright idea to advance the notion

that both Porter *and* Cullion should be considered suspects in the Las Vegas murders until our DNA sample could rule out either one or the other. This gave me some leeway to go after the little rat—at least until the San Francisco Police Department could secure some cooperation from Angela Porter.

She wouldn't release a single one of Shoo-fly's effects for DNA testing, and Al Bowers couldn't get a judge to issue a search warrant for them. Mrs. Porter claimed Shoo-fly took everything with him. No one wanted to dispute with the well-connected heroine of the Marina district.

My Mexico theory didn't last too long. Shortly after Wanda Buckley's demise, I began checking everything on record about scheduled transportation out of the states and into Mexico. But that led nowhere. Then Cullion's car was found abandoned in San Diego about three weeks after he left San Francisco, which led everybody but me to decide that I was right about him being in Mexico. I took it as a very obvious diversion. Mickey was too devious to point the way south and actually go there. Now I was sure he'd gone to Idaho.

To my mind, that was confirmed when we found out Shoo-fly had Mickey's driver's license and other identification. He tried to use it in Phoenix, where the bank manager got suspicious. That meant Mickey had no I.D.—unless he was able to procure a fake. If he had none, he certainly wouldn't be leaving the country.

Fake I.D. or no I.D., Mickey was sure to be using a new name. At this point, I suspected what he longed for most was a feeling of security. And what would generate security better than a place associated with fond memories? I decided to take a closer look for relatives or old friends in Idaho.

CHAPTER 49

YACHT FOR SALE

PARTY GIRL. Kristi Darnell would bristle when they called her that on E! or in the media. It's what they say on Page Six of the New York Post when they mean prostitute. She may have been stuck with it, but she never accepted it.

She met him in South Beach. Yes, it was at a wild and woolly SoBe nightclub, but she still didn't deserve to be called names. That was totally unfair. After all, she was a model and actress, and she had the credits to prove it. Just local commercials for the acting jobs, but she got modeling assignments all the time. And South Beach modeling gigs are the real thing—great production values, top professionals, good money.

Kristi was at Nikki Nikkita with friends, hanging out, the night she noticed the good-looking older man watching her. She figured he was about thirty-two. He was very well-built with long black hair, a full beard, and the most intense blue eyes she had ever seen. Like most guys on the scene, he wore shorts, flip-flops and t-shirt. Kristi never had the least suspicion about his real identity until he told her who he was later on. Shoo-fly was only a tabloid story to her then, one of those things you read about but never dream you'll be part of.

While he sat at the bar, he must have noticed Kristi's return looks. As she came back to her table from a trip to the ladies' room, he intercepted her and chatted her up, taking pains to keep it light and flirty. Often drawn to older guys, Kristi didn't hesitate to take the drink he offered. Soon after, the girls she was with just laughed when she blew them off and left the club to go out to dinner with him. They thought he was cute too. The name he used was Sam Davidson.

"Is that your real name, Kristi Darnell?" he asked as they left the club.

"What a question!" she said. "Did you think I'd give you a phony name?"

"You're an actress—I just figured you might have made it up. That happens, right?"

"Not so much nowadays, but yeah, it's a stage name. My real name is Christy Gore. I hated that. So I changed the spelling of the first name and took the last name from an actress my grandfather used to talk about."

"Who would that be?"

"Linda Darnell. Ever hear of her?"

"No, but I'll bet anything the world will hear about you, Kristi."

Sam was a real flatterer. There was no question he was feeding her a line, but it was done with a friendly smile and she couldn't take offense. Forward motion was his overall method to break down her defenses. At the same time, he was polite and considerate. If she asked him to slow down, he would smile and apologize, but before she knew it he was making another move. She figured when you really like a guy, you don't mind that.

Even today, Kristi refuses to talk about sex with Sam—she thinks it's totally intrusive that reporters and other complete strangers want to know what he was like in bed.

"Just because they have nerve enough to ask," she complains, "they act as if you owe them all kinds of private information."

She fell fast. On that very first night, Kristi knew she was in love. From the beginning, Sam had a way of making her feel completely protected and wanted. She must have needed that. Only twenty-two at the time, she was often unsure of herself in that world—casting calls, modeling, even the SoBe nightlife could make her feel lonely and insecure.

Sam moved into her apartment in nearby North Beach soon after they met. He had a little money, and they shared expenses. He talked about being a dropout from corporate life on the West Coast, looking for fun and a better way to make a living.

"I broke my butt on my last job, Kristi. I put my heart and soul into it only to find out I was the only one who cared. That's not going to happen to me again."

"What do you think you'll do now, Sam?"

"Well, there's a tremendous number of boats and yachts down here. I'd like to start out working for a broker."

Pretty soon, he was making friends down at a marina on Alton Road. A man named Lou Loiselle had a yacht he wanted to sell, and Sam was helping him get it into shape. Mr. Loiselle liked to take his boat out into the Intracoastal, but he was getting older and didn't want to bother with the yearly upkeep any longer.

Kristi and Sam would laugh about Lou from time to time because of his mannerisms and his habit of wearing certain clothes whenever he took the bridge— always the blue blazer with the brass buttons and his white captain's hat with the black peak. She thought he was like a father figure to Sam—except that he was so obviously effeminate.

Besides working on the restoration, Sam did a nice job of describing the yacht for sale. He had fliers printed up and posted around town. Lou was content for the time being to try for a private sale, and he promised Sam a percentage if they sold it before he signed with a broker. Sam saw to it the yacht was listed in boating magazines and posted on likely Internet sites.

Modeling jobs kept Kristi busy just then, so most days she and Sam would wake up at different times and not see each other until late afternoon. She began to notice how moody he could be, and that it did no good to try and draw him out. He could be extroverted and a lot of fun, but in several ways he was the most self-contained person she ever knew.

Kristi would come home to see him lying on the bed, stripped down to briefs and a t-shirt. He wouldn't say a word unless she spoke first. Hands under his head, he would stare at the ceiling, an empty look in his eyes. If she got up the nerve to ask what he was thinking about, he might not even answer.

One rainy Tuesday a conversation they had alarmed her, had her wondering if Sam should look for professional help. Kristi had come home early after an aborted photo shoot, and Sam was stretched out on the bed in that peculiar way of his.

"Are you day-dreaming, honey? You're so quiet just lying there."

"Not day-dreaming, no. Sometimes my thoughts are jumbled up and I think better lying down."

"What's on your mind, Sam?"

"A lot of things. There are people who mystify me, you know? Some folks have a way of judging you while they talk to you, like they're ready to accuse you of something. And you can only wonder about it because they haven't said anything, it's what you're reading in their eyes and their manner."

"Is there someone in particular you're concerned about?"

"Maybe. I don't want to say. I want to put it out of my mind, that's why I'm trying to relax."

"Don't you want to talk to somebody about this? It would bother me something awful to feel that way."

"I'd rather you didn't think about it, Kristi. I'll work through it. I don't want to blow it out of proportion and get mad. It's not good for me to get angry."

There was something terribly disjointed about the way he was thinking; she could tell he was trying to control it by slowing down. He spoke softly in a kind of edgy monotone. Kristi didn't feel afraid for her own safety, but she was afraid of what he was capable of doing. He was very strong, and when his mood turned, you could see his jaw set and his muscles flex. Combined with the overly intense stare she sometimes noticed, the effect was unnerving.

Sam had very few clothes for a guy who was in corporate life previously. He mentioned donating most of his business wardrobe to charity. He did have one rumpled, dirty suit when he first moved in. After a trip to the cleaners, it stayed on its hanger in the bedroom closet. He never wore it that she could recall, just held on to it as a memento of his life in San Francisco. Kristi came to the conclusion that his career had been a terrible failure, and she wondered why he would want a reminder of that.

In truth, she was beginning to wonder about a lot of things. When Sam told her Lou Loiselle had died suddenly, she didn't understand why it wasn't in the newspapers.

"Lou's from Fort Lauderdale, Kristi. I'm sure it's news up there. He was just visiting Miami, living on the yacht."

"But you're still going out to the Marina most mornings, Sam. What's that all about?"

"Lou's sister called and told me to keep showing the boat, babe. She wants it sold."

Kristi said nothing to Sam, but Lou had told her he had no family left. Could she be mistaken? No, she was sure. And it must have been her curiosity—or her dread—that brought her down to the Marina early one afternoon a few days later.

She only half expected to find Sam there, but he was gone. As she walked down the pier toward the yacht, she ran into Cindy, a middle-aged lady whose husband owned the boat across from Lou's. They conversed for a bit while the bright sun warmed her shoulders and the boats rocked gently in their slips.

Cindy mentioned that no one had seen old Lou for a while. She claimed Sam didn't know where he was either. Kristi tried to cover her confusion with a shrug and a smile that wouldn't jell, then cut her visit short before Sam could show up. What could this possibly mean?

When she got up the nerve to question Sam about it that evening, his look was hard, his manner impatient. Then he laughed. A sharp, rasping laugh, full of sarcasm. For the first time, Kristi felt afraid of her lover.

"I killed him, Kristi. I killed the old fag. He was drunk, he tried to touch me, wanted to blow me is what he said. I grabbed the fire extinguisher and bashed his faggot head in."

As he spoke, the look on Sam's face ranged from hot anger to indifference.

"We sailed around to the Gulf," he told her. "The water was calm, sky clear. A perfect day, really, until Lou had too much to drink. Then he got way too friendly."

He related it as if it were a story he heard somewhere—some filthy, contemptible anecdote that he'd just as soon forget.

Why didn't she run? Why didn't she tell somebody? Instead, she wanted to take care of it for him. For the only guy who had ever made her feel safe and wanted, Kristi thought she could return some of that. To this day she struggles with it—becoming an accomplice to the murder of a dear old man she knew and liked. It seemed to her the greater good was to protect the man she loved—this murderer she couldn't seem to part with.

"What did you do with the body, Sam?" she asked.

"I weighted him down with chains and an anchor and dumped him in the Gulf. I don't think there'll be a problem. He's not coming back up."

When they made love that night it was consuming, feral. The fear she felt jacked up the excitement of his lovemaking while she told herself he would never hurt her. No, not his Kristi.

She lay in his arms afterwards while he talked about people crossing him, how it made him feel. Suddenly, she thought about that Dolce & Gabbana suit he never wore hanging in the closet. She remembered the stories in the tabloids about the well-dressed killer Shoo-fly out west, the big, good-looking psycho murderer who sliced people up and ran away. It was then she knew she was in love with a man beyond all redemption. How could she get away from him? Did she even want to?

He must have sensed her suspicions about him. The next evening, as they strolled the beach barefoot, he confessed that his real name was Sam Porter, the one the newspapers called Shoo-fly.

Everybody knows the story. He narrated every detail as if confession might help him understand what he was. She heard about the fuzzy, spotted vision, the rush of wind in his ears, and the labored breathing. When he got that way, he couldn't stop until he saw the blood flow.

Kristi stopped working—the pressure she felt was paralyzing. Her life had changed, and she wanted to leave Florida. But she couldn't take that first step. Sam seemed to be watching her for signs of—what?—

betrayal, help.

Before long there was a newspaper story by Rupert McAllister that said Helena Swann wasn't in San Francisco any more, had left for parts unknown. He seemed to hint she might be in Europe.

"No . . . not Europe," said Sam. "They're wrong about that. She has relatives up north."

Kristi felt her heart sicken when he talked about those women—his wife and her notorious sister Helena. Angela was the one everybody thought was so regal, so perfect. Did he want to go back to her? This was jealousy, and Kristi knew it.

"No, not that. I could never face her again."

"You're in love with her, aren't you, Sam?"

"No. I never loved Angela. But she loved me, and she helped me when no one else would. I owe her a lot."

Kristi felt her face flush and her eyes fill. Sam drew her close, stroked her face with a big hand, and stared through her with his searchlight gaze.

"Do you love me, Sam? I have to know how you feel."

"My feelings for you are very strong, Kristi, and I want to be with you when I get back."

"Get back? What do you mean? Where are you going?"

"I can't tell you, baby. It'll take about a week. I'll call before I come home."

But he never did.

CHAPTER 50

CALL IT A HUNCH

LIEUTENANT VIEJO

LIKE I TOLD MY WIFE, it's not rocket science. Just pulling out a map and looking at it for a few minutes, I had some ideas where Shoo-fly was headed. I couldn't know his ultimate destination, of course. That was locked up in that degraded brain of his.

Since our boy had been spotted in both Reno and Phoenix, he must have passed through Las Vegas, even if he didn't stop and say hello this time around. And now if he wanted to disappear into Mexico, he would beat it down to Tucson after Phoenix and try to cross at Nogales. Or, if he figured he needed to get out of Arizona right away, he'd go from Tucson to Las Cruces and El Paso in Texas. From there, he could cross into Juarez.

Still, if he didn't have a new ID, he wouldn't try for the border. And if we were to hear of him anywhere like San Antonio or points east, then the game was over for Mexico. So, after this genius-level lawman prognostication, I made some phone calls to my colleagues in those towns I mentioned. After that, I sat back and waited. It wasn't in him to be quiet for any long spell of time. We'd hear of Shoo-fly again—oh yes we would.

~ ~ ~

Norm Partridge called me on a Thursday in August. I remember because I had an appointment to take Ellen's old Cougar in for the three-thousand-mile check-up she had been putting off for about twelve thousand miles. Greatest gal you ever want to meet, Ellen is, but she tends to neglect the car maintenance.

Norm Partridge is the chief of police in Austin. His buddy Vic Moreno in San Antonio was someone I had been in touch with.

"Vic tells me you're the guy I need to talk to, Viejo."

"What can I do for you, Chief?"

"Well, we just shut down a fake ID operation and the Vietnamese guy that run it wanted to plea bargain with some information he had. I wasn't too happy about it, but the D.A.'s office tells me the guy is a first-time perp who won't do no time anyway."

"Sounds like you got somebody for me, Chief. Mind telling me who it is?"

"I can only *wish* I had him, Viejo. I'd surely be into my fifteen minutes of fame about now if I did. It's Shoo-fly. The little Vietnamese guy tells us he fixed up your boy with top grade ID. Seems like he goes by the name of Sam Davidson now. And he sprouted a beard since you saw him last."

After the conversation with Partridge, I pulled out the map again and saw that Mexico was out of the question. Unless he doubled back, Shoo-fly would more likely be headed towards Houston and New Orleans. After notifying detectives in both cities, I didn't really see what more I could do. I had asked everyone to keep Shoo-fly's new ID away from the media for now. At least until we'd had a shot at locating and nailing him.

Still, I had a feeling there was a loose end somewhere and it nagged at me until I thought of Brad Styles. Right away, I called and told him I needed to talk to Angela Porter. Like everybody else, I could only speculate where Helena Swann had hidden herself, but I had the uneasy feeling that Shoo-fly might not be finished with her.

Styles ran through every misgiving he could think

of to put me off, until I got a little hot under the collar.

"I *know* Mrs. Porter doesn't speak to cops, Styles. And I *know* she doesn't answer questions about her sister, either. But dammit, I think Helena Swann is in danger!"

"How so, detective? I can assure you no one has been told where she is."

"I see. You've kept it quiet, huh? Like you kept Mrs. Porter's pregnancy quiet?"

"Now listen, lieutenant! You can't talk to me like that!"

"Styles, I'm sorry. That was out of line. But I have new information on Sam Porter I want to talk to Mrs. Porter about. Along with advice about protecting Helena Swann."

He didn't like it, but Styles set up a three-way conversation an hour later with Angela Porter, himself and me. As always, her voice had a certain refined melody somewhere between compassionate good humor and sad reflection.

"Why do you think my sister is in danger, detective?" she asked.

"Call it a hunch, Mrs. Porter. I don't have direct evidence. What I want you to know hasn't been released to the media. Your husband was last seen in Austin, Texas. He's using an alias—Sam Davidson. The route he's taking seems to rule out Mexico as a destination. He may very well keep on this southern track, but you have to understand anything is possible."

Both Styles and Mrs. Porter fell quiet.

"Please notice I'm not asking where she is," I said. "Just consider how well protected she is and take as many precautions as you can."

Angela Porter was gracious in thanking me for my concern about her sister. I couldn't help thinking that I had almost as little concern for Helena Swann personally as I had for Shoo-fly. Legally she was clean—so far—but morally I figured they were two of a kind.

A few weeks later, the Florida leg of our saga exploded when a body surfaced in the Gulf of Mexico and came ashore on Pine Island. It can take a long time to identify the bloated, half-eaten mounds of human flesh that wash up from time to time. In this case, however, the dental records of a missing person named Louis Loiselle led to a positive identification.

When the police were notified who the corpse was, their investigation linked two people to poor Mr. Loiselle—Kristi Darnell and Sam Davidson. One of them was still in Miami Beach, accompanied by her lawyer at every questioning, but the other had taken off for parts unknown.

CHAPTER 51

DESIGNATED DRIVER

IT PROMISED TO BE an interesting summer for Ivan Chitworth, although his passion for the dramatic went unfulfilled at first. Ivan was dying to talk about hosting a genuine femme fatale at Dismas Cottage. Regrettably, he found himself required to be evasive and coy about the glamorous blonde from California.

Secrets, like the one he was sworn to keep about Helena's identity, were almost unheard of among his friends. The crowd he ran with came from the very best families, complete with trust funds.

None of them deigned to work, except on their tans. They lived for certain social events, played tennis and golf, and patronized the arts. Gossip was the very air they breathed.

Newport was mostly a summer thing for his clique. The autumn diaspora to New York and Connecticut was an annual event around Labor Day. Ivan was one of the few exceptions, having become a year-round resident when his mother sold the New York apartment to move there permanently.

Helena's first surprise for him was her new look. She was blonde now with short, tousled hair. It was more on the order of a makeover than a disguise—still, only a close friend or relative would recognize in her the dark-haired temptress whose photos were a standard feature of the tabloids stocked in your local supermarket checkout aisle. Furthermore, she kept a low profile in Newport. Ivan had expected to introduce her to one or two select friends, but she stayed aloof, intent on keeping herself under wraps. When she

233

couldn't avoid giving a name, she called herself Helen Chitworth.

Even so, she was the same streetwise gal with the sophisticated taste and sharp wit. Chastened now, perhaps, and wary of calling attention to herself, but it was Helena nonetheless. As she relaxed into the lazy Newport rhythm, she and Ivan spent many hours together at tennis, on the beach, or just strolling Cliff Walk. He kept the talk light—it's a specialty of his—but despite his best efforts, there was a haunted quality in her mood from time to time.

And what could be more natural than that, after all she had been through? Ivan wasn't privy to her innermost thoughts and could only look at the events in Las Vegas and San Francisco through the prism of his own understanding. By attending her sister Angela's wedding, however, he did experience one part of the saga at first hand.

When Angela introduced Ivan to Sam back then, he nearly wilted under that cold blue stare. Sam was polite, jovial even, but that look of his went right through Ivan, who thought he could see the big man's opinion of him formulate on the spot—queer. Anyhow, what Sam thought didn't bother him in the least. Ivan was perfectly aware of how he came across to people and what they said about him. His assessment of Sam was also instantaneous—dangerous and sexy beyond words. *You go, Angela*, he thought.

A few weeks after the wedding, the whole sorry scandal broke. By then, Ivan was back in Newport. The police had connected the dots, and everybody was reading Rupert McAllister's sensational report about the murders in Las Vegas and San Francisco. McAllister was the one who called Helena Delilah in his dispatches.

Right away, Ivan's mother asked him not to talk to

anyone about the family connection to Angela and Helena. He thought she was afraid of the publicity. Later, he realized she was thinking ahead. When Helena asked to stay with them for a spell, they were able to tell her that people in Newport were unaware of their relationship.

Newport, of course, has seen no end of scandal and mayhem over the years. People especially recall Claus and Sunny Von Bulow and the dark deeds done right around the corner and up the street from the Chitworths on Bellevue Avenue. Until the day she died years later, poor Sunny lay unavenged in a coma—a persistent vegetative state they called it.

Anyhow, the day arrived when McAllister slithered into Newport, determined to meet with Helena. On the night she agreed to see him, Ivan offered to remain home with her. But her expression told him she had other plans.

"Oh, Ivan honey, do go out tonight. I told McAllister that he and I would be alone."

"Why would you want to be alone with one of your worst enemies?"

"He knows I'm here, and he must want something. So why not meet him on a friendly basis? Depending on what he's after, I may gain some leverage."

It didn't make a lot of sense to Ivan, but he didn't press her. Helena was used to living life on a pretty big stage. She pondered her every move and thought over the motivations of everyone she interacted with. He couldn't begin to understand that way of operating—it struck him as positively Byzantine.

So while Helena was preparing to greet McAllister, he met his friends at eight o'clock in the rooftop bar at the Terrace Hotel. It's called the Blue Moon—a popular spot in the summer months. The serving area is backed up to a brick wall, which they overspread with a striped canvas awning. The rest of the rooftop is surrounded by a balustrade and filled with seating and a small dance floor.

Ten or twelve couples occupied a number of the tables that night. Ivan and his friends—four in all—sat at the bar. It was early and therefore quiet: no one dancing, no one drunk. A reggae band was playing with the kind of shuffling beat tourists seem to like at summer resorts.

Dusk was falling. From the bar, they could look out and see the old residential and commercial areas that crowd the hill leading down to the harbor. In the fading light, church steeples and the masts of sailboats were just discernible against the rippling shine of water.

Ivan must have been quiet for a spell because Jack Hamel asked if he were feeling all right.

"I'm fine, Jack," he said. "Do me a favor, though. Tell me if the big guy at the end of the bar keeps looking this way."

"You can't be serious, Ivan," he laughed. "This is Newport, after all. People do not come here to cruise."

"More's the pity. But keep an eye on it for me, will you?"

"Sure, if you say so."

As it turned out, Ivan was right. The guy had longish hair and a full beard. He was dressed in shorts, a print shirt worn outside and fisherman sandals. Ivan took him for a contractor or construction worker who just dropped in for a beer. But he was nursing it, that beer, and soon Jack confirmed that he was looking their way now and then, more often than you'd expect.

Ivan asked himself the usual questions. Who's he looking at? What does he want? Could it be someone who knows me? Should I try to find out? Because he felt awkward when it came to approaching people, he turned to Jack.

"What do you think? Should I go over and talk to him?" he asked.

"Ivan, he looks like a real bruiser, you wouldn't want to be wrong."

"Well, you know I'm not bold enough to make a play, anyway."

"I suppose you could walk by and say hello if you catch his eye."

"Uh-huh. And then what?"

"On your way back from the men's room, smile and say 'How 'bout those Red Sox?'"

Ivan and Jack cracked up at that.

"With my luck, he'd be a Yankee fan," he said.

Before long, he had mostly forgotten about the big guy while the four friends made conversation about Jack's weekend in New York. Later, when Ivan thought to turn around and check, the man was gone.

Just before ten o'clock, everybody decided to pile into Jack's car for the forty-minute drive to a dance club in Providence. Everybody except Ivan, that is. He didn't tell anyone, but he was anxious to find out what Rupert McAllister wanted with Helena. If he went to Providence now, they would be out until two in the morning. In which case, he'd have to wait until breakfast to learn what the Tabloid King had to say.

Jack, Tony and Marc said goodbye and left a few minutes before Ivan, who stayed behind to chat a moment with the bartender. When he slid off his barstool and headed for the exit door leading to the elevator, he inhaled the night air and realized he was pleasantly buzzed. Not drunk, just a little high.

Not having a designated driver, he'd have to be careful on the short haul back to Dismas Cottage. He would get there before ten-thirty, and if McAllister hadn't left, he'd go to his room and wait until Helena was free.

When the elevator doors opened onto the lobby, Ivan walked straight ahead to the front entrance. On his left were the bell captain's station, the front desk and a small sitting area. And there he was. The big guy occupied an armchair and was talking with a woman in her early twenties. Ivan's eyes met his as he passed by. He interrupted his conversation, smiled and said hello.

Ivan felt the color rise to his cheeks. There was no call for him to be embarrassed, but something had clicked in the back of his mind. The voice, he thought, something about his voice. He would have liked to pull out his glasses for a better look, but no, that would be way too obvious. Besides, he was too vain to wear them unless the need was dire.

He paused on the hotel's front steps a moment before crossing the street to the parking area behind the old Jewish cemetery that faced the hotel. A soft amber glow haloed the Victorian-style street lamps and spilled onto the shops lining the avenue. The night air was mild and damp. A mist was beginning to drift in from the harbor.

Traffic was light. Ivan crossed and was into the lot before hearing footsteps. Startled, he wheeled around and spotted him. The level of light from the street behind him obscured the man's features, but he recognized his form in the semi-dark.

He laughed and spoke up right away.

"Sorry. Didn't mean to scare you. The name's Dave. I'm parked here too."

He had stopped where he was, about six paces away, probably feeling that would enable Ivan to settle down.

"Oh, that's okay," Ivan said. "I guess I got spooked. Don't let me keep you."

He passed into the lot, car keys in his right hand. Smiling pleasantly, he kept an eye on Ivan as he approached a light-colored Ford Torino.

"Listen," he said, "I'm not from around here. Could you tell me how to get back to the bridge?"

While he gave directions, Ivan watched him open the front door on the driver's side and pull something off the dashboard. He shut the door and held up a map.

"Maybe you could show me the way on this," he said. "I want to get back to I-95."

Ivan took an end of the map, pointed out their approximate location, and showed him the route to the highway. They were standing close and he became flustered, wondering if—maybe hoping—the big fellow would say something or make a move.

With a downward tug, the map disappeared, replaced by a gun peering into Ivan's face. He was being shoved backwards, against the nearest car. He started to resist, but looking down the gun barrel took the starch out of him. A big hand was square against Ivan's chest with a lot of weight behind it. Instinctively, he had grabbed the man's wrist, but now he released it and put his arms back, palms outward at the level of his head. Surrendering.

"Good boy, Ivan. Take it easy and stay quiet. Everything will be all right."

He wanted to ask how he knew his name, but was afraid how his voice would sound. Ivan didn't want to beg for mercy or sound like a wimp, so he waited for the man to speak again. His breathing was tortured, and soon he would hyperventilate if he couldn't relax. It was then he realized why the voice was familiar. *Oh sweet Jesus*, he thought. *It's Sam, he's here for Helena.*

"Okay, Ivan, you're gonna get up now. That's it, nice and slow. Hand over your wallet and your cell phone first, then go over to my car and get in the driver's side."

Ivan could barely think straight, but he surmised Sam wasn't attempting to rip him off. He must want the wallet for the address—to find out where Helena was staying. When they both were in the car, Sam handed him the keys.

"Drive out of here slowly and turn left onto the avenue."

"Helena's not in Newport," Ivan said. "She's in Boston."

Sam grinned and nodded. "We'll just have to wait for her to come back, won't we? I know what—we'll take a ride along Ocean Drive and talk. That's down this way, right? The bartender told me it's real scenic. I'll bet you know it."

He was right; Ivan knew it well. The drive meanders along the southern tip of the island, a mix of large estates, coves, beachfront and parkland all nestled against the open sea. At night in the moonlight, it's majestic, dark, and nearly deserted.

"Why don't you just let me go?" Ivan asked. "I told you she's out of town. I can't do a thing for you."

Snarling now. "Yes you can, faggot! You can shut up and drive!"

That made him mad and he wanted to say so, but Sam's eyes were hard and his voice was commanding. Ivan shut up.

"Leroy Avenue . . . Tell me exactly where that is from here." He was looking in Ivan's wallet as he said it.

He wanted to lie, but they'd be passing Leroy in a few moments, and he might easily see the street sign.

"It's up ahead to the left, just a few more blocks," he said.

"Good. Thanks. But pass it by, we're going to Ocean Drive, remember?"

For a moment Ivan felt relieved, then worse than ever. If Sam wasn't after Helena and they weren't headed toward Dismas Cottage, what did he have planned? He supposed he wouldn't be long in finding out.

Despite the mildness of the night and the open car windows, Ivan's face and arms were covered in a glaze of sweat. His heart had finally stopped pounding at about the time they passed Marble House, but his hands still gripped the wheel tightly in an effort to control his shaking.

Bellevue Avenue turns to the west at Rough Point, where the old Doris Duke estate sits sprawling like a medieval castle above Cliff Walk. The moon was high as he made the turn, investing the scene with a kind of pallor that did little to illuminate the darkened roadway.

Two more turns in the road brought them on to Ocean Drive. Ivan could hear the surf slapping the sand at Bailey's Beach as they headed west again. In a few minutes, he saw the sign for King's Beach.

"Pull over here," Sam said. For emphasis, he dug the gun barrel into to Ivan's ribs.

He made him get out and stand in the roadway next to the car door. The beach wasn't visible from there, just the sandy, rocky path leading to it. Gun in hand, Sam got out of his side and slammed the door shut. While he waved Ivan toward him, he walked to the back of the car.

"Open the trunk," he said.

Ivan fumbled with the keys. He didn't try to use the remote because he couldn't read the symbols well enough in the dim light. Sam was getting impatient.

"C'mon—c'mon Ivan. For Christ's sake!"

Again Ivan said nothing. Finally, he inserted the right key and the lid sprung open. Sam took the car keys from him and told him to stand away a few paces. Keeping one eye on him, Sam shoved the gun under his waistband and groped around in the trunk, pulling out two lengths of rope and a shovel.

He turned to Ivan and smiled as he closed the trunk.

"We're going up that path to the beach. You've been real good so far, and I appreciate it. You're not gonna get hurt if you just cooperate. So cooperate."

Ivan didn't believe him at all, although he wanted to very badly. If he had felt steadier, he might have run into the trees and brush along the opposite side of the roadway, but he was too nervous and would have stumbled and fallen. The last thing he wanted to do was make this killer angry.

Sam pushed him along the path, and his breathing grew more strained. He staggered forward, stinging sweat gushing into his eyes. His already weak vision grew blurry.

"What the hell . . . you drunk, Ivan?"

"I . . . can't see too well," he said.

"Not to worry, we're almost done. Stand over here facing the water, and put your hands behind your back."

While Sam tied his hands at the wrists, Ivan stood looking out to the ocean and the stars. *What I wouldn't give to be sailing out there*, he thought. He so wanted to stay calm. But what was the shovel for? What was next?

"Face down on the sand, Ivan. C'mon, son, do it now!"

His mind was racing as Sam trussed him up from behind, ankles to wrists. Sand was getting into his mouth and nostrils, and his breath came in short and painful bursts.

"The house keys, Ivan, I forgot to ask for your house keys."

He laughed when Ivan didn't answer, probably guessing he couldn't speak to tell him what pocket they were in. When he found them and stood up, everything was silent for a long moment.

Facing the wrong way, his cheek against the gritty sand, Ivan couldn't see him. Oh God, he thought, is he pointing that gun at me? When the silence continued to lengthen, Ivan began to hope Sam had gone. But again he wondered what that shovel was for. Finally, what he remembered after was the sound—*CLANG*—and the blinding pain in his head. The night enfolded him.

CHAPTER 52

A LITTLE TOUR

JUST BEFORE NOON on Wednesday morning, an old friend dropped Helena off at Dismas Cottage after their tennis date. Exhausted, she was anticipating a hot shower and a quiet afternoon at home. Entering through the *porte cochère* at the side of the house, she put her racket in the big foyer closet and was stripping off her sweaty headband when Aunt Claudia glided into her field of vision. She was holding her hands at waist level, wringing them slowly. The look on her face was Yankee tragic. Her mouth was drawn down, and her brows were crinkly with concern.

"What is it, darling?" Helena asked.

"Rupert McAllister called and left a message. I told him I hadn't seen you in years, but he just laughed. Oh, what a terrible man!"

"What was the message?"

"I told him it was foolish to leave word since you would never get it. He said, 'Tell her to call me at the Hyatt Regency,' and he hung up."

Like the replay of a bad dream or the recurrence of a dormant malady, the name Rupert McAllister filled Helena with dread. For the moment she managed to suppress her fear in order to console her aunt. She told her there was nothing to worry about.

"But Helena, dear, what will you do?"

"I have to think about it, but I'm inclined to call him. Apparently, he knows I'm here. If it were just a fishing expedition, he wouldn't be right here in town, would he?"

"I suppose not, but what good will it do to confirm

that for him?"

"That's what I have to think about. If he knows I'm here and I *don't* call, he'll surely write one of his awful stories and everyone will know. Maybe there's something I can do for him in return for keeping quiet about my stay here . . . for now, at least."

"Oh, Helena, are you sure?"

"Please don't worry, Aunt Claudia. I'll think of something."

"Well," she sighed, "would you like of cup of tea, dear?"

Her aunt's offer of tea was an all-purpose remedy, the universal answer to life's woes. While Claudia sought out her maid in the kitchen, Helena went off to shower and change clothes. It gave her a chance to think things through.

The mental ease she was cultivating during those weeks in Newport had already suffered a setback when Angela called her about taking further "precautions." Lieutenant Viejo from Las Vegas had urged her to do it. Two days ago, a newspaper story linked the body that washed ashore in Florida to Sam. And now, here was that slimeball McAllister come to torture her.

It was clear she must talk to him. On the phone, he was unctuous and condescending. With the utmost politeness, Helena invited him to come and visit at eight-thirty the next evening. She made no demands or preconditions. She wouldn't try to negotiate until they met.

"Thanks so much, Mrs. Swann, for agreeing to see me," he said.

"My pleasure, Mr. McAllister. There'll be just the two of us. We'll have drinks and a nice chat."

"Delightful! I'm so looking forward to it."

I'll just bet he is, she thought. Aunt Claudia wouldn't present a problem. She had made plans weeks ago to leave for Boston, where she'd be for a few days with a friend in Back Bay. Helena figured to ask Ivan to stay away for a few hours, so she could meet McAllister alone. As a matter of fact, that was Ivan's routine on Thursday anyhow.

With that settled in her mind, she began to chew over every event and every emotion of the past few months. The only comforting thought was that Sam was unlikely to look for her while so many people were on his trail. His best bet had to be a big city where he could blend in, or perhaps some truly isolated spot where someone could hide him.

Despite Helena's assurance of security in Newport, every newspaper story about Sam's odyssey from San Francisco to Miami put her in agony and renewed her sense of dread. How much of all this was about her? And why did she think these thoughts, why did every new felony and murder seem to form a link in a chain that bound her to him? Part of the problem was that she never made a mental break with him. Even now when she dreamed about lovemaking, Sam's was the face she was kissing, his the body pressing against hers.

Dealing with McAllister would mean answering questions on every aspect of the family scandal. He would certainly want to hear it all—her relations with Sam, what she thought about Angela's pregnancy, what she knew about the Las Vegas murders, the status of her engagement to Brad. Although she planned to tell him as little as possible, somehow she had to extract his promise not to reveal her whereabouts. Maybe she could trade some future exclusive for his cooperation now.

She certainly wouldn't say anything to him about the jealousy that consumed her whenever her sister's pregnancy came to mind. Oh, *she* didn't want to be pregnant, the thought of having Sam's child was truly dreadful. But her sister's due date! Counting backwards, Helena realized the child might have been conceived that last morning in San Francisco, just before they all came down for breakfast. *After most of the night in my bed*, she thought, *the bastard probably impregnated his wife..*

~ ~ ~

By the time McAllister arrived the next evening at eight-thirty, Helena felt in command of her emotions and quite sure she could handle him. She brought him into the living room and asked him to sit on the striped silk Biedermeier sofa, while she occupied higher ground in a straight-back armchair. There was a low mahogany serving table between them. They exchanged the usual pleasantries, and he gushed about the amenities of Dismas Cottage. Helena smiled and nodded through this without commenting, just as she had seen Aunt Claudia do a hundred times.

"Will you take a drink, Mr. McAllister? A brandy, perhaps?"

"Why yes, Mrs. Swann, I will. If it's no trouble, that is, and if you'll join me."

"No trouble at all. And of course I'll join you," she said, crossing the room to the liquor cabinet.

There was a silver tray on top of the cabinet. She took out two snifters and a bottle of cognac from the bottom shelf and put everything on the tray. As she carried it back and placed it between them, she pointed out a box of cigars on the table.

"If you'd like one, I'd be pleased to light it for you," she said. "I won't join you, of course, but it gives me pleasure to see a man enjoy a good cigar."

"Thank you, Mrs. Swann. Absolutely delightful!"

He selected a cigar, took up the little cutting tool, and clipped off the end. Helena was ready with a lighter, and he pulled in the smoke with a sucking noise until the ash end glowed red. While he watched, she poured a few ounces of cognac into the bottom of each snifter. From his demeanor, she could tell he was succumbing to the ritual. Very few men can resist this sort of thing. The ones who do resist *won't* be charmed, she knew, and must be dealt with very differently.

"Now I know we have business to discuss, Mr. McAllister, but I'm hoping we can get to know each other first. If we can talk off the record, that is. I'm very mistrustful of journalists after what's happened."

"I should think you would be. And I do apologize for the sensational aspects of my articles. That sort of thing grows out of not having access to the right people. One can't expect a balanced reportage when the only source willing to talk is a Mickey Cullion."

Now this was utter bullshit. The reportage was tabloid style because the story was tabloid fodder, pure and simple. But Helena went along.

"Yes, I see what you mean," she said. "You know, Rupert, I'd like it if you could tell me a little about yourself. You're from London, aren't you?"

That got him started. She knew that middle-class Brits are often uptight with upper-class Americans. They feel out of place and will insist on acting superior unless one disarms them with a modicum of respect and an easy manner. Once she had accomplished that, the evening went very well indeed.

He filled her in on his background, and she let him know a few things about her life as an aspiring actress in New York after college. Although she made sure they were still off the record, she felt certain this was information he already had by now.

"Did you ever appear in a lead role, Helena? You certainly have the presence for it."

"No, I was neither a very successful actress nor a very good one. Casting directors seemed to like me for parts like 'Vassar girl' or 'socialite bitch.' I never had a big role, never the kind of success you've had in journalism."

"Really, you know, this story has made me. I can't point to much else."

"Well, you've done a lot with it."

"I suppose so. I've had some luck and I've been resourceful. But there have been . . . well, frustrations."

"Such as?"

"You'll pardon me for saying so, but I'm angry that your sister and your fiancé have continued to stonewall me."

"How could they do otherwise, Rupert?"

"Don't you see? Their side of whole affair could be on the record. All the nasty conjecture would not have been possible."

At least he was consistent with that line of claptrap. But it was ludicrous. When you go 'on record,' there is that much more room for disputation and innuendo. At this point though, Helena thought it was time to deal with him.

"Well, I'm sure that your business tonight is to ask *me* to go on record. Still, I don't believe it's time."

"When *will* it be time, Helena?"

"I'm not sure. Right now I feel trapped. You've found me despite my precautions, and I'm at a disadvantage. If you tell the world about me, Sam Porter will know where I am."

"There will be no reason to do a thing like that if you can help me a little."

"Rupert, I'm not a rich woman like my sister Angela, despite what people think. Would my story be worth something?"

"Of course. It could be worth a great deal."

In a few minutes, Rupert McAllister was in an expansive mood. He had a verbal agreement with

Helena for an exclusive interview on her involvement with 'Shoo-fly' for a sum she would negotiate with his publisher. A written agreement would follow when negotiations were complete, and she would not be interviewed until Sam Porter was in jail.

His business taken care of, Rupert let his guard down with a cognac refill and was relating details of the Reno and Phoenix stories that had never made it to print.

"That cowpoke he trounced in Reno was the real thing, Helena—pure Texas," he laughed. "A big rangy lad with leathery skin. And that broken nose! He never had it set properly, just pushed it back into place as best he could!"

McAllister was having a good time making fun of people involved in the case, and Helena egged him on. But she had to wonder why he thought she would ever tell her story to someone so likely to treat her the same way.

"As soon as I found a publisher for the book version," he said, "I began collecting eyewitness accounts whenever possible. Some of them have been unsuitable for the newspapers."

"Why? What do you mean, Rupert?"

"Well, everyone knows that Shoo-fly peed on the bank manager's family picture. But I have affidavits from six customers who were there that day. Each of them said very nearly the same thing. First, they were terrified by his display of temper. Second, after he turned the place upside down, he pulled out the biggest uncut willy they had ever seen."

While Rupert laughed at his own cleverness, Helena smiled demurely. And she changed the subject before he could ask question one about *her* familiarity with Sam's anatomy.

"Why don't I give you a little tour of Dismas Cottage

before you leave?" she suggested. "You've seen only the rooms downstairs."

It was ten-thirty, and she wanted to be rid of him. Ivan would be back soon, and she was expecting Aunt Claudia to call from Boston. As they ascended the staircase, she decided to point out some features of the house, show him the library, and call it a night.

The corridor at the top of the stairs comprised a kind of portrait gallery depicting several generations of Chitworths. While Helena related a few details from the life of Pardon Chitworth of the Mayflower Compact, she heard a noise downstairs which she assumed was Ivan opening the front door.

Steering Rupert into the library, she closed the double doors behind them. Ivan knew she didn't want them to meet, and this would enable him to get upstairs to his room unseen. So Helena was rather annoyed when the doors opened again, just as she was showing Rupert an original New York edition of the works of Henry James.

Helena's breath caught, and she felt her knees almost give way when she turned and saw it was Sam framed by the doorway, not Ivan.

First, there was a moment of grace and confusion while she processed the beard, the long hair, the substandard clothing. McAllister turned to look, puzzled at first. Then his face drained of all color.

Sam's dreadful gaze was like a knife attack dealing her one quick thrust before fixing itself on Rupert, who threw up his hands and began screaming in a high-pitched wail. When Sam pulled the gun from his waistband, the poor man begged for his life.

"Pl-e-e-e-ase don't kill me!" he screeched. "Pl-e-e-e-ase!"

He caught up with Rupert in front of the fireplace and slapped him left-handed across the face, again and again, all the while degrading him with insults. He tried to stagger away, but Sam seized his collar and kicked him to the floor. As Rupert turned a forlorn and tear-streaked face towards him, Sam stepped on his chest, raised the gun, aimed, and shot—a look of rage-filled contempt on his face.

Helena had inched herself over to the doorway. Just as she heard the gun discharge and saw Rupert McAllister's tortured face explode into flying shards of bone and brain, she slipped outside and slammed the doors shut. Because of all the rare books, the library was fitted with locks that secured it from either side. By the time Sam understood he'd have to shoot his way out, she would be gone from the house.

He was kicking at the doors while Helena raced downstairs and out the front entrance. The telephone was ringing as she left. Dashing through the grounds to Leroy Avenue, she heard two gunshots from the house. Sam would be coming after her now.

If she could get to the corner of Bellevue Avenue before he saw her, he'd have to guess whether she turned south towards Marble House or north towards Memorial Boulevard and the town. Her lungs hurt from the exertion, and her breathing was labored, but she pushed on as hard as she could. That she might fall and let him catch up was a terrible, nagging fear.

At the corner of Bellevue and Leroy, Helena looked back, dreading what might be there. Was he in sight? No, not yet. *Which way now*, she thought, *which way?* She slipped around the street corner to the south and rested a moment, crouching down by the hedge at the boundary of Chateau-sur-Mer, oldest of the large estates on the avenue. Just a little farther south were the entrance gates—she ran to them and hid behind a tree inside the grounds. From that vantage point, she kept her eyes on the corner of Leroy, where she hoped to observe Sam's approach as he came up to Bellevue.

Time expanded the way it does when fright has hold of you. If only she had her cell phone! Nerves taut and legs trembling, she knew she wouldn't get far if she had to run again. As she strained to listen for footsteps, the only thing she heard was her own breathing.

If Sam had gone towards town, she thought, it might be possible to sneak back to Dismas Cottage. She darted back to the driveway gates and peeked around them to see if he had turned north on Bellevue. Her eyes took in the glamorous heart of Newport: the endless row of Victorian street lamps, the gilded age mansions buffered by wrought-iron gates and high protective bushes—all bathed in misty moonlight. Still no sign of Sam.

Oh, but there he was—not thirty feet away—he had somehow scrambled to the *other* side of Bellevue. When he saw her, a smile stole across his face and reached his eyes. It occurred to Helena he looked . . . more handsome than ever. But he raised the gun and took aim.

In blind panic, she stumbled out to the sidewalk before righting herself and dashing back up the driveway toward the chateau. She meant to run a zigzag pattern, but the shot he fired came whining past her ear and drove her straight ahead.

Moments earlier, she had seen a flash of light when she peeked around the gates. No, it wasn't the flash from his gun. Perhaps she was beginning to hallucinate a little from nervous tension. There it was again, and again. Now, still running, Helena heard another shot— followed by searing pain. She dropped to her knees on the asphalt and fell face forward, panting.

Sam was shouting her name in a rasping voice she hardly knew.

"Helena! Helena! I'm here, bitch!"

There were other voices too, and a barrage of gunshots. Pop! Pop! Pop! And still she saw the flashing lights. Then footsteps came pounding up the driveway, and she tried to brace herself—for death. In that last, crucial moment, however, it just didn't seem to matter as much as she thought it would.

"Miss? Are you all right?"

A young policeman with schoolboy looks knelt beside her. She understood the flashing lights then—his squad car.

"I've been shot," she moaned.

"An ambulance is on its way, ma'am. I'll stay here with you until it comes."

"Did you catch him?" she asked.

"We took him down, ma'am. He's dead."

"Oh."

"He mumbled something before he died. It sounded like 'Delilah.' Do you know who that is?"

Helena averted her face. "No," she whispered. "No I don't."

CHAPTER 53

AN UNNAMED COLLABORATOR

LIEUTENANT VIEJO

RUPERT MCALLISTER WAS MOURNED by many who didn't know him, and by few who did. His girlfriend, with the help of a ghostwriter, finished his book and dedicated it to his memory. As you might have guessed, neither of the Sharples sisters cooperated.

Funny how a story peters out after the saturation point is reached. The book sold well enough, but it was no blockbuster. My wife enjoyed it, though, especially the part about me being an upright lawman with a strong face and a gone-to-seed athlete's body. Everybody kids me about that. Just another cross to bear, I guess. In police work, you get used to it.

I can only recall one more tabloid headline you might get a charge out of, this one from the Boston American when Helena Swann went back to San Francisco:

NEWPORT NOTABLES CLOSE MURDER MANSION

It seems that Shoo-fly 'fans' stalked the grounds on days the garden paths were open to the public. As a result, the Chitworths moved from their home temporarily and hired a security firm to monitor the place until the crush died down.

By then, with Helena Swann back in San Francisco and Mickey Cullion tracked down, I was preparing my files for storage. Well, you can stow the paperwork, but that doesn't mean you can put the case out of your mind. I still think of Shoo-fly and Helena a lot. I always will. For me, they're the male and female versions of human evil, or whatever else you might prefer to call it—sociopathological mentality, maybe.

They didn't have horns or tails, and they both had qualities you could understand and perhaps admire. His ego and determination to succeed propped him up until his potential for lust and brute force burst through. At the end, only violence and tortured desire could sustain him. Helena was a lot more subtle, but like the black widow spider I've heard her compared to, she was deadly as well, even deadlier than the male. When it came to survival, after all, who was left? She was seduction and entrapment personified, and she prevailed, after a fashion.

If you're wondering how the Newport police showed up at the right time, I had worked things out with them at Angela Porter's request. Helena, Ivan, and Mrs. Chitworth could call for help anytime day or night, and the police would react immediately. In addition, the three of them were required to be in touch with each other every evening by eleven o'clock. One of them, usually Helena, called the police to let them know everything was all right—or to report if someone was out and hadn't checked in.

The duty sergeant in Newport was responsible for contacting Dismas Cottage in case there was no report by eleven. If no one answered when he called, two silent squad cars would be dispatched with the presumption there was trouble at the house and that Shoo-fly was involved.

Well, it wasn't a perfect system, but it helped. Angela Porter sent me a handwritten note a while back to thank me for saving her sister's life. Now that bothered me when I recalled that my scheme was also responsible for her husband's death. I never expected any thanks from Helena Swann. Needless to say, I didn't get any.

I used to see Pedro Brunetti along the Strip from time to time, but no more. He must have a new source of income, because he got out of the P.I. business and went home to Mississippi. I hear he goes by the name of Pete Brown down there. Now if I were a betting man, I'd make a hefty wager that he was the leak McAllister had depended on for some of his stories.

My final conversation with Pedro took place right after the book came out. I was coming out of Harrah's, and I spotted him just ahead of me on the Strip. We were both on foot, so I hustled to overtake him.

"Pedro, have you seen McAllister's book? I just read it."

"Why yes, lieutenant, I picked up a copy the first day of publication. You might know his death couldn't stop that book."

"You were treated very well, I thought."

"And fairly, too, don't you think?"

"Sure, Pedro. But you know, I've always had this suspicion there was an unnamed collaborator besides McAllister's girlfriend and the ghostwriter. One of those 'sources close to the investigation' knew way too much. Know what I mean?"

"Oh, I don't know, lieutenant. There may have been a leak somewhere, I suppose. A police officer, perhaps. But as far as my involvement with the case, I think of the verse in II Timothy: *I have fought a good fight, I have finished my course, I have kept the faith.*"

Well, I let him have the last word. But he knew what I was getting at. What a character!

POSTSCRIPT I

THE EAR OF JEALOUSY

MICKEY CULLION

ME, I WOULD'VE JUST AS SOON been fishin' all along. But I was the type to do anything for a friend. I may have said that before, so sue me.

Lately, I've been thinking of the mountains and cool streams around Teton Valley where the fish still run good, and you can spend a whole day soakin' up sun and fresh air and maybe catch a trout if you're lucky. The sort of life I knew as a kid and went back to over the years whenever I could.

No job? No prospects? No problem. I'd just go back to my uncle's cabin in Teton Valley. It was a pattern of mine, until I met Shoo-fly in stir and went on that damn safari of ours—cowboy crap, bars, fights, and then Vegas and fuckin' Frisco. Maybe you know that assholes who live there hate for you to call it Frisco. Well, they can sue me too.

You probably figured out that I couldn't hide forever, and you'd be right. When Bailey Viejo—where the hell did he get that name, anyway?—tracked me down, I was up there in the cabin, just like he guessed I would be. He found an old schoolteacher of mine and pumped her for information. Old schoolteachers don't forget much.

I may not have been smart enough to hide out from the law for long, but I was smart enough to lawyer up right away. They had me on embezzlement charges in

Frisco, which was a no-brainer. But if I kept my mouth shut they could only threaten about accessory after the fact in the Vegas murders and accessory before in Wanda's case. And Mickey Cullion knows how to keep his mouth shut.

Helena Swann had done me a favor after all. I figured it was no empty promise she made to have me taken down if I told everything. But that game goes two ways. I could put her ass in a sling for being Shoo-fly's bag woman after Wanda Buckley's murder. No one would have to know, as long as I didn't have to face a murder charge. I told the truth about the money, except that I claimed Shoo-fly gave it to me a week *before* Wanda died. Only Helena could screw me up there, which ain't ever gonna happen.

The law is like most institutions I've run across. What they don't know don't bother them much. And they manage not to know what they don't want to deal with. It's only *people* got scruples about right and wrong—institutions just got rules.

I had to cop to what happened in Wanda's hotel room on account of my DNA was all over the place. SFPD believed my story that it was a twofer with Shoo-fly needing to get rid of me as much as Wanda. Which was true as far as it goes. I sure as hell didn't tell them I had practically set the old lady up for him. Naturally, I played dumb about Shoo-fly's moves back in Las Vegas. I doubt if Viejo bought that, but I guess I carried it off.

There's no doubt it was Brunetti got into my head about what a chump I was, made me start thinking my life through. When the case ended and Shoo-fly was dead, I could still hear them bible verses Pedro quoted while he was recording my story. After a while in stir this time, I joined an evangelical group and got into bible study with a pastor who comes around twice a month. Hard to believe, right?

Now I kind of shudder and sweat when I read certain verses—because the whole story of Shoo-fly was told a long time ago. Any kind of right teaching and right thinking in my life, and I would have known as soon as it all began. It scares me now I realize how much there is to answer for. Shoo-fly's first fix for a problem was to hurt somebody, kill if he thought he had to. As for me, I was always there to help, even when I knew it was wrong.

Whether or not Helena Swann ever appeared on the scene, it was always gonna end in disaster. She may have juiced up the story real good, added some class. But she was only icing on a poisoned cake. I brooded over both of them for months, told everybody who would listen how much I hated them. It helped me gin up a sweet case of the poor me's—until I had to give it up for a bad job. Pastor Jim tells me I gotta work on myself, nobody else, and I believe him. Hard as I try, though, those two are stuck in my head like bad thoughts—the pals who helped me get where I am.

Yesterday, I was lying on my bunk reading through the Wisdom of Solomon, when I came across a verse that reeked of Shoo-fly and Helena: *The ear of jealousy heareth all things.* Both of them had some kind of sonar that homed in on everything said or done by the other, imagining they were being crossed . . . or cheated on. But that doesn't explain how I fit into the pattern. My coffin gets nailed shut in II Peter, where all three of us are hammered in the kind of language I understand best: *The dog is turned to his own vomit again; and the sow that was washed to her wallowing in the mire.* I'll be damned if that doesn't say it all. And I suppose I'll be damned if it does.

Still, I'll be back on the street again in a few months. Maybe things will be different this time—you can see I've already changed some. And if you're interested, my reputation with the shiv keeps the wolves away from me in here. No more boyfriends for me in the slammer. I'd have to be nuts.

POSTSCRIPT II

JUSTICE PURE AND SIMPLE

HELENA SWANN

I RECUPERATED IN NEWPORT for some months under the care of Ivan and Aunt Claudia. Despite the loveliness of the town, I carry the image of crows with me when I think of Newport now. There was a time when the name Newport called up thoughts of lazy summer afternoons, the glint of sun on salt water, and the splash of laughing bathers diving through the surf.

But now I think of crows. Flocks of them would gather in the autumn twilight and fill the sky outside my bedroom window with their sinister forms. To me, they were harbingers of death and the void. I felt my flesh creep at their raucous cries, as they flew from one stand of beech trees to another. Copper beech trees, morbid dun skies, and black, shiny crows—this mix will forever signify the colors of autumn in New England for me.

Sam was dead, the story of Shoo-fly was over, but I still lived on. Time and again, I think about it—the horror, the pain, the excitement. Will I ever know how to understand him? As a human being, definitely not. I once described him as a force of nature, and maybe that comes close. He was a hurricane tearing through lives, causing us all to react to him and each other in unpredictable ways. He was the center of the universe for a short, violent term. We couldn't see or hear anything else. Then he was gone, used up, and we were left to wander in the wreckage. A hurricane doesn't have a soul, it just happens.

My life in San Francisco is mostly serene these

days. I only wish people didn't whisper behind my back when I'm in public. Oh, I suppose they can't help themselves. How ironic it must seem to them that Angela takes care of me now. You see, the gunshot nicked my spine and left me crippled. In a wheelchair now and always, dead from the waist down. More irony there, I suspect.

The hardest pill to swallow was Angela marrying my Brad. Yes, I'm bitter about it, as I have always been about my life. But I see things clearly now. It's justice, pure and simple, and I have to recognize that, even as it pounds me into the ground.

I'm sure you know I have a nephew. Brad adopted the little guy without publicity. Both mother and dad take great pains to shield him from the press. I pity Angela having to tell him about his natural father, even though that's a long way off. Somehow she'll manage it perfectly; she always does. Brad is absolutely marvelous with him—he's just the kind of dad I imagined he would be.

When I play with Justin (there was no question of naming him after Sam), I inevitably think of everything that led up to his birth. Brother, it's a lesson in justice to know that son of a bitch Sam got the better deal. Instantaneous death for him, pain and utter humiliation for me. To top it off, I live surrounded by his wife, his spawn and the man who used to love me. Oh, I'm Delilah, the Black Widow, the Dragon Lady—take your pick. Whatever Sam was, he's dead now and beyond all opprobrium.

You know, they call me his *femme fatale*, but I wonder. Who's to say he wasn't my *homme fatal*? When I think it through, that's how I see it, how I feel it. There's no need, I suppose, to tell you I don't like how this story ends. But I can't rewrite it. I'm a fatalist now, I don't believe in alternative endings.

POSTSCRIPT III

A MOTHER'S TEARS

KRISTI DARNELL

IT JUST WASN'T IN MY POWER to turn what I felt for Sam into hatred. Even though he could do precisely that, as he did with Helena Swann. The one thing I could do was distance myself from the scandal. So I moved away from Florida four years ago, as far as I could get from reporters and police detectives. I've a new life now, and a new identity that I guard jealously.

Still, the thought of him up north, in a pauper's grave probably, bothered me no end. If that's how it was, I figured I could buy a small marker with his name on it. A man's life, even Sam's, has to be worth some reminder that he walked the earth, despite the things he did. The simple fact was I still cared. So I made a sort of pilgrimage to find out where he was. I had to know, I had to see with my own eyes.

Since I'm a gal of the modern South, I'm sure you'll realize New England was strange to me. When I arrived there, Newport struck me as more akin to Europe than anything I had known back home. If you need a southern reference, though, think of it as a chilly Charleston, or as St. Augustine without the palm trees.

It was hard to believe a little town could have so many cemeteries. I guess that has something to do with how old the place is—founded in 1639. The streets abound with references to early American history and

Revolutionary War heroes. Every other building is a plaque house.

I had no intention of making a fuss up there, but I did call Ivan Chitworth. He told me about his rescue the night Sam died. It seems an old fellow out for some night fishing came along just as the incoming tide was starting to pool around poor Ivan. From the look on the man's face, he must have thought he had found a talking baby whale in the darkness. You can't help but laugh at Ivan's way with a story.

When I got around to asking where Sam was buried, Ivan hesitated. So I ginned up my courage and told him my story. Finally, he took pity and gave me directions to the little historical graveyard I had to locate.

Clifton Burying Ground is tucked away in a colonial neighborhood on a steep, winding hill behind the public library. There are dozens of weathered slate gravestones (so many of them for children!) from the 1600's, representing the oldest Newport families. When I stepped through the opening in the white picket fence, my eyes teared up. About five yards away was a new stone in the Chitworth family plot. Thank goodness he isn't in some Potter's Field, I thought. Then I read the inscription:

Samson Porter
Beloved Husband of Angela

That took my breath away. Beloved husband. He violated her trust, tore through her life, destroyed her family and still she called him that. There had to be something right about this man for two good women to love him so. Psychotic, charming, handsome, evil, thoughtful, lonely and lost. Those are the facts about him and despite everything, two of us remember the good.

I've promised myself never to intrude on Angela Porter Styles, but I want more than anything in life to know what her son Justin is like—the first child of Samson Porter. I'm the only one in the world who knows he has a half-brother, my precious little son.

Under that bleak New England sky, little Sam stood by me at the grave with a frightened look, wondering at his mother's bitter tears.

= = =

Thank you for reading.
Please review this book. Reviews help others find New Pulp Press and inspire us to keep providing these marvelous tales.

If you would like to be put on our email list to receive updates on new releases, contests, and promotions, please go to **NewPulpPress.com** and sign up.

ABOUT THE AUTHOR

Paul McGoran lives in Newport, Rhode Island. In his life before fiction, he was a laboratory technician, a Russian language interpreter for the U. S. Navy, a career marketing executive, a management consultant, and a day trader. As a writer in the crime genre since 2005, his inspiration comes in equal parts from spending way too much time watching black and white film noir from the forties and fifties, and from reading way too many hard-boiled detective stories.

A short story by Paul, *The Thanks You Get*, was published by the U.K. webzine PulpPusher. His next novel, *The Breastplate of Faith and Love*, will revisit several characters featured in *Made for Murder* -- and will indtroduce a series P. I. named Stafford Boyle. Currently, Paul is working on a third novel that will bring Stafford Boyle back to his hometown to solve the revenge murder of the bully who terrorized his childhood.

Be on the lookout for a volume of Paul's short crime fiction, *Paying for Pain*, available soon from **NEW PULP PRESS**.

NewPulpPress.com

www.ingramcontent.com/pod-product-compliance
Lightning Source LLC
Chambersburg PA
CBHW060526260626
47161CB00003B/783